NOW FOR THE GOOD NEWS

PENGUIN BOOKS

UK | USA | Canada | Ireland | Australia
India | New Zealand | South Africa | China

Penguin Random House Australia is part of the Penguin Random House group of companies whose addresses can be found at global.penguinrandomhouse.com.

This edition published by Penguin Books, an imprint of Penguin Random House Australia Pty Ltd, in 2024

Text copyright © Planet Ark 2024

Design by Rebecca King © Penguin Random House Australia Pty Ltd

Text written by: Jordan Artery, Laura Chalk, Sarah Chaplin, Niki Foreman, Pamela Jolly, Alejandra Laclette, Emma Lucey, Jennifer McMillan, Rachael Ridley, Nicholas Scaltrito, Liam Taylor and Tamanna Wadhwani.

Illustrations by: Rebecca King and Sarah Wiecek.

The moral right of the author has been asserted.

All rights reserved. No part of this publication may be reproduced, published, performed in public or communicated to the public in any form or by any means without prior written permission from Penguin Random House Australia Pty Ltd or its authorised licensees.

Every effort has been made to acknowledge and contact the copyright holders for permission to reproduce material contained in this book. Any copyright holders who have been inadvertently omitted from acknowledgements and credits should contact the publisher and omissions will be rectified in subsequent editions.

Printed and bound in China

Penguin Random House Australia uses papers that are natural and recyclable products, made from wood grown in sustainable forests. The logging and manufacture processes are expected to conform to the environmental regulations of the country of origin.

The production of this book is carbon neutral.

A catalogue record for this book is available from the National Library of Australia

ISBN 978 0 14377 958 2 (Trade Paperback)

penguin.com.au

We at Penguin Random House Australia acknowledge that Aboriginal and Torres Strait Islander peoples are the Traditional Custodians and the first storytellers of the lands on which we live and work. We honour Aboriginal and Torres Strait Islander peoples' continuous connection to Country, waters, skies and communities. We celebrate Aboriginal and Torres Strait Islander stories, traditions and living cultures; and we pay our respects to Elders past and present.

NOW FOR THE GOOD NEWS

PENGUIN BOOKS

CONTENTS

THE GOOD NEWS

THE GOOD NEWS

THE GOOD NEWS

To the future generations of our beautiful planet,
may you remember us not for what we didn't do,
but what we did, as you set out to do even better.

PLANET ARK

GET WIRED FOR THE GOOD NEWS

Do you ever find that you just can't take in any more bad news, and that bad news or fake news just seems to come at you from every direction? From your smartphone, from TV, from the radio, social media, emails . . .

As humans, we are wired to be attracted to drama, which often comes in the form of bad news. But what if the drama was overcoming a challenge? In all stories, from fairytales to fantasy to real-life, and everything in between, there is always a challenge that the main character overcomes. And this book, dear Reader, focuses on how we are overcoming some of those challenges and hitting you with some **GOOD NEWS**!

Who is our main character in this story, you ask? Well, it's our very own Planet Earth.

And who are Earth's friends and enemies? Well, the answer to both of those questions is: we are.

Read on to discover how **GOOD NEWS** can take over the world, and what you can do to keep the **GOOD NEWS** coming.

Blue Planet

BLUE PLANET

Look at our Earth. Isn't it beautiful? It is no secret that water makes up two-thirds of Earth's surface and yet our oceans are the part of the world we know the least about. They are so vast that it's impossible to know how many species live there (we have knowledge of only about 9% of the oceans' species) and only 20% of the oceans are mapped (we know more about the shape of the surface of the moon than about the shape of the bottom of the oceans!). What is clear is that the number of species are likely to be shrinking because of human interference. Many of our human actions hurt the watery environment and its inhabitants, but the full extent of this is unknown. And so how can we protect what we don't fully understand? What we *do* know about the oceans is that they are *hugely* important to the health of our whole planet.

WHAT WE DO KNOW

Our oceans are one large body of salt water that covers 71% of Earth's surface and holds about 96.5% of all the water on Earth. Humans recognise five different bodies of water that make up the global ocean system, which are the Atlantic Ocean, Pacific Ocean, Arctic Ocean, Southern Ocean and Indian Ocean.

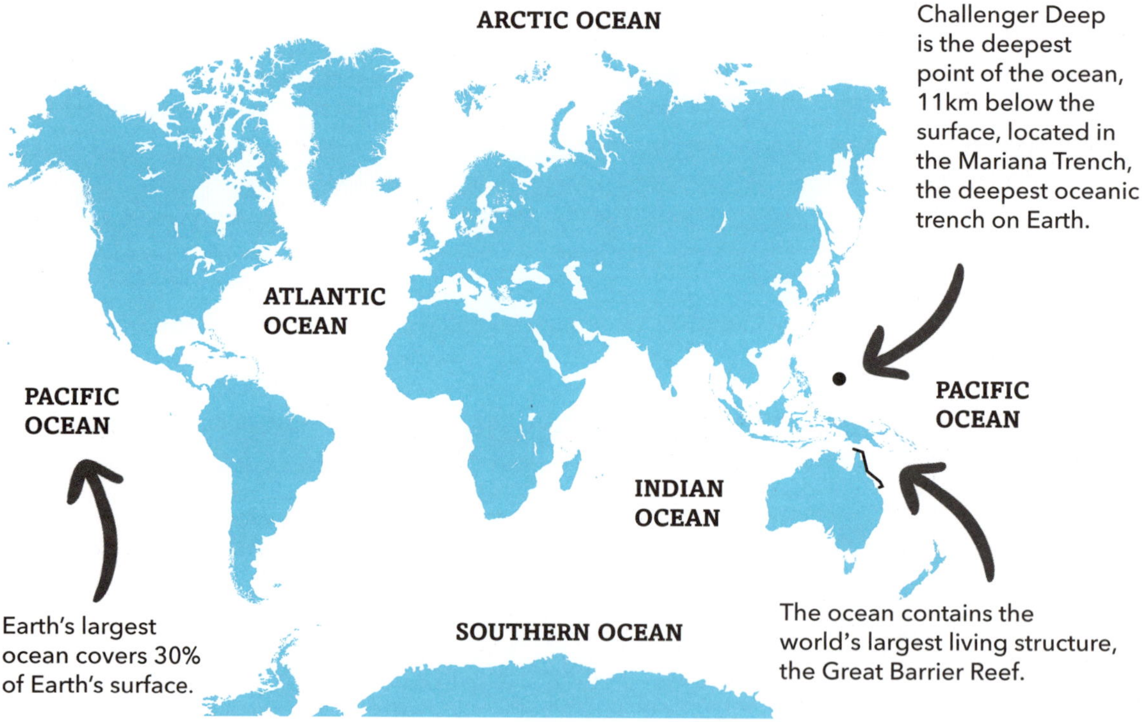

ARCTIC OCEAN

ATLANTIC OCEAN

PACIFIC OCEAN

INDIAN OCEAN

SOUTHERN OCEAN

Challenger Deep is the deepest point of the ocean, 11km below the surface, located in the Mariana Trench, the deepest oceanic trench on Earth.

Earth's largest ocean covers 30% of Earth's surface.

The ocean contains the world's largest living structure, the Great Barrier Reef.

We rely on the oceans for our survival as a species. The oceans produce more than half of the oxygen that we breathe, mostly by plankton, drifting plants, algae and bacteria. Other critical services the oceans provide to us and other living species include: providing the primary food source for half of the global population, being the largest source of water (which all living things need to survive), and dictating the planet's weather and regulating climate change. They also support human activities such as transportation (90% of global trade is carried by ship), a renewable energy supply (through the tides and waves), the creation of many medicinal products and, of course, recreation.

INTERCONNECTED

Much like on the land, in the oceans there are warm regions and cool regions and microclimates. There are also mountainous areas and flat plains. And as on land, there is a huge diversity of life in the oceans. Just as the rivers and beaches feed into the sea, so the sea feeds back to the land. This interconnectivity is crucial to our planet's survival, and because of this, our understanding of oceans' health is also key to that survival.

THE WATER CYCLE CONNECTION

The water cycle is just one example of how the ocean and land are interconnected. It shows the non-stop movement of water between the oceans and the land that is key to Earth's health. Unfortunately, it's a cycle that is disrupted and polluted by human interference.

1. Sunlight warms liquid water in the oceans, which evaporates to become a gas in the atmosphere.
2. The gas rises over land and condenses (cools) to form clouds.
3. As the clouds cool, the water turns from gas to liquid and falls as rain and snow back to land.

4. The water runs over the land into rivers that carry it back out to the oceans.

WHAT PROBLEMS DO OCEANS FACE?

Have you heard of the greenhouse effect? It is the natural phenomenon that makes Earth liveable. So-called greenhouse gases (such as carbon dioxide and methane) in Earth's atmosphere act like the glass of a greenhouse and help retain some of the sun's heat, which makes Earth warm enough for life to survive. But human actions have resulted in more greenhouse gases being released into the atmosphere, causing an enhanced greenhouse effect that traps more of the sun's heat on Earth, which leads to a warmer planet and warmer oceans.

THE GREENHOUSE EFFECT

4. Less of the sun's heat escapes Earth's atmosphere.

3. The thicker atmosphere that surrounds Earth traps more of the sun's heat, making Earth warmer.

2. More greenhouses gases, such as carbon dioxide and methane, create a thicker atmosphere around Earth.

1. Human actions, such as burning fossil fuels like coal and gas to create electricity, release more greenhouse gases into Earth's atmosphere.

MORE GREENHOUSE GASES . . . WHAT DOES THAT MEAN FOR OUR OCEANS?

1. The oceans absorb a lot of the excess carbon dioxide that has been released into the atmosphere due to human actions, but more carbon dioxide makes the water more acidic (ocean acidification), which makes it unliveable for some marine life.

2. A warmer Earth means warmer oceans and a rise in sea levels. This is because when cold water warms, it expands and takes up more space. Warm water also causes sea ice to melt, which adds to the amount of water in the oceans, making sea levels rise further as well as reducing the size of Arctic ice (which is frozen ocean) for animals such as polar bears.

3. Warmer ocean water affects the ocean currents, which in turn affects Earth's climate and carbon-dioxide systems – because cold water absorbs and holds more carbon dioxide than warm water. The ocean currents are like a global conveyor belt, circulating water around the globe in a 1000-year cycle. They are driven by cold water that sinks to the sea floor, depositing some of the carbon in the sea floor where it remains locked for millions of years, and then flowing as a deep-ocean current until the water warms and rises to the surface again. Less sinking cold water due to warmer oceans also affects the amount of oxygen-making algae in the water, which is what so much of ocean life relies on.

THE OCEAN CURRENTS

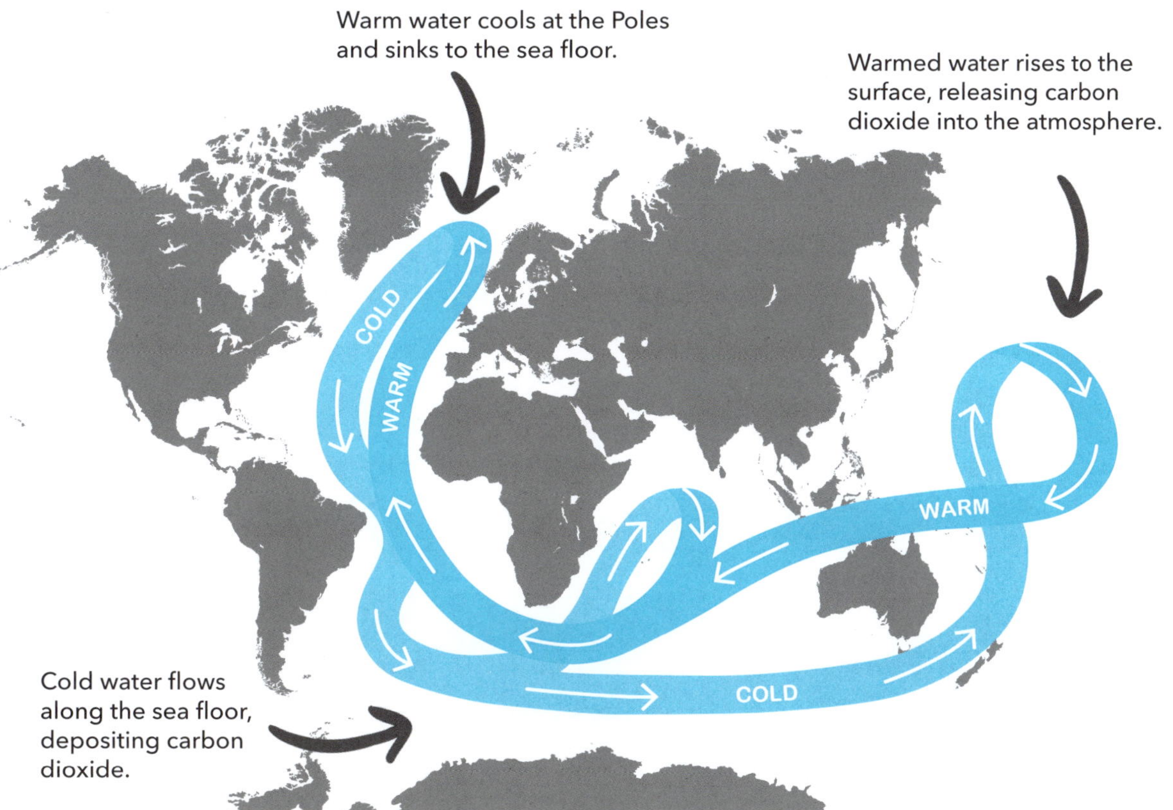

OTHER WAYS WE MUCK UP OUR OCEANS

Overfishing: The total amount of vertebrate sea life (marine animals with backbones, including fish) has reduced by more than a third since 1970, mostly due to humans excessively fishing areas of the oceans until fish stocks are significantly depleted.

Destruction of ocean habitats: This includes coral bleaching (when colourful coral turns white) caused by marine heatwaves, and fishing methods such as trawling and use of dynamite that wrecks the natural habitats on the seabed. Coastal development that increases the number of people in contact with the ocean also affects the local marine environment.

Plastic pollution: Our discarded plastics are contaminating water and killing ocean life – an estimated 1.7 million tonnes of plastic ends up in the oceans every year.

Other pollution: Chemicals like fertilisers and pesticides flow from the land into the waterways and oceans; antibiotics and other chemicals are released into ocean waters through aquaculture (fish farms); and our use of fossil fuels releases mercury, which is highly toxic, into the atmosphere that then makes its way into the sea and can poison marine life.

“THE OCEAN IS OUR GREATEST RESOURCE, AND WE MUST TAKE ACTION TO PRESERVE IT FOR FUTURE GENERATIONS.

Jacques Yves Cousteau, oceanographer

Blue Planet

THE GOOD NEWS
SEABIN

They say the simplest ideas are the best, and the Seabin proves it. Floating on the water's surface and automatically collecting floating debris, the Seabin is a cross between a garbage bin and a pool skimmer. In the places it has been installed, it continuously cleans the harbours and waterways of some of the staggering 1.7 million tonnes of plastic waste that enters our oceans every year. But it also does so much more . . .

THE JOURNEY

The Seabin's life began with two surfers, Andrew Turton and Pete Ceglinki, who, in the waves off the east coast of Australia, were unable to enjoy their surf due to the view, which looked something like this:

Irritation turned into conversation, which eventually turned into an idea: the Seabin. The duo upskilled themselves by watching YouTube videos on welding and sewing, and the original Seabin was created in 2015.

TESTING THE WATER

After some early testing of the Seabin prototype in the French marina La Grande Motte, the Seabin was then trialled in Sydney's harbour in 2020 over a 12-month period, and the results exceeded expectations. It collected so much rubbish that it was terribly clear just how much trash was in the oceans. The ripples that the Seabin trial made attracted investors with an environmental conscience, and today it is a much wider project that both turns a profit for its creators and acts as a not-for-profit charity in order to invest back into the Seabin communities.

HOW DOES IT WORK?

The Seabin is strategically positioned upstream in harbours and rivers according to factors such as tide, wind and current that bring the debris to the seabin. A solar-compatible water pump sucks the surface water (and any waste in it) into the floating device. The water passes through the catchbag and is pumped out the bottom of the bin, leaving any rubbish, microplastics, fuel, oil and other harmful contaminants trapped in the catchbag. The catchbag can hold up to 20 kilograms of rubbish before it needs emptying. Once collected, the rubbish is then recycled or otherwise disposed of in a safe way.

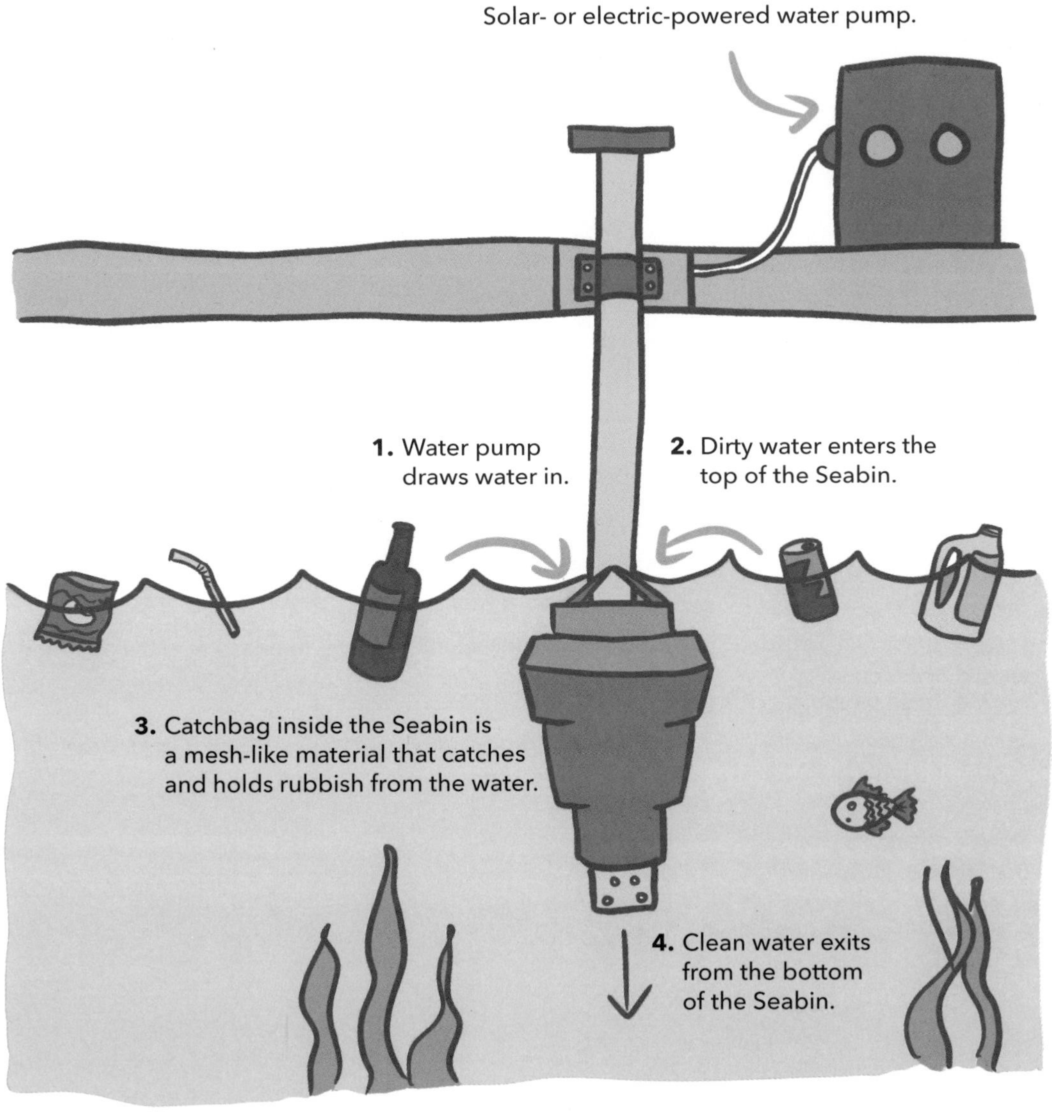

Solar- or electric-powered water pump.

1. Water pump draws water in.

2. Dirty water enters the top of the Seabin.

3. Catchbag inside the Seabin is a mesh-like material that catches and holds rubbish from the water.

4. Clean water exits from the bottom of the Seabin.

KEEPING IT SIMPLE

While the concept for the Seabin is simple, the project details have been quite complex. For instance, finding the right material for the catchbag that ticked each of these boxes took years, needing much trial and error. It is no coincidence that the Seabin is now into its sixth version, with each design catching tinier pollutants, or being more environmentally friendly in how it is powered or in the materials it uses.

Catchbag Requirements

- ✓ allows water to pass through it but catches viscous (thick and sticky) fluids such as fuel and oil
- ✓ collects microplastics and microfibres as tiny as 1mm plus the big stuff
- ✓ the material it's made from is planet-friendly

BEYOND THE PRODUCT

The Seabin project does more than just collect the litter. Following its Whole Solution strategy, the Seabin team is also researching where the litter comes from, logging the trash type on a global database for comparison with similar waterways, and seeking to find solutions that involve prevention as well as clean-up.

THE WHOLE SOLUTION

Data monitoring:
Measuring marine health through the amount of debris and pollution each Seabin collects.

Data analysis:
To help industry and governments form policies to prevent future pollution.

Identifying the causes:
By finding where the pollution comes from, help those contributing to the pollution to change their behaviour.

Debris interception:
Getting to the litter and disposing of it properly before it reaches the ocean.

Community programs:
School and community education programs to inspire behavioural change, such as stopping littering and reducing the use of plastics. What can *you* do?

MEASURING

To help measure and analyse the increasing amounts of data it receives on a daily basis as more Seabins are installed in waters around the world, the company has produced its own Pollution Index (PI), which helps to rank the local water's cleanliness and general waterway health based on how much litter is caught by the Seabin in a single day. The index's scale goes from 1 to 11, with 1 being only 1 piece of plastic found in more than 50,000 litres of water, and 11 being the most polluted waterway, with plastic found in every single litre of water.

Using this index, Sydney Harbour has a PI cleanliness rating of 5.

THE SEABIN FUTURE

Seabin aims to operate in 100 cities around the world by 2050.

It has already been taken up by cities in more than 25 countries around the world. Not only does the Seabin itself get its hands dirty by actually helping to clean the oceans, the company's data-recording systems help to provide local councils and world leaders with real facts in real numbers that make pollution measurable and comparable – and also make the resident city accountable.

Accountability means taking responsibility and is key to saving our planet by helping humans change their behaviour. One day, hopefully, we won't need Seabins.

Blue Planet

THE GOOD NEWS

THE OCEAN CLEANUP

Seabins are one way to clean up harbours and waterways, but what about all the plastic already out there in the oceans? Dealing with that colossal amount of rubbish requires some serious science and engineering, which is exactly where the crew at The Ocean Cleanup come in . . .

WHERE IT ALL BEGAN

When Dutch inventor Boyan Slat went on a scuba-diving holiday in Greece, he was horrified to see more plastic bags than fish in the sea. So he set himself a mission: to rid the world's oceans of plastic. In 2012, with just a few hundred dollars to his name, he founded The Ocean Cleanup, which has now grown into a global organisation of more than 120 employees from more than 30 countries. The Ocean Cleanup team has a big dream – to clean up 90% of all floating plastics. To achieve this, they have two main objectives. The first is cleaning up all the plastic that's already out there in the oceans. The second is intercepting plastic before it reaches the oceans.

CLEANING UP

The Ocean Cleanup crew have already started their work with an incredible piece of engineering that collects and removes plastic from the ocean surface. The system is constantly being updated and the current System 03, nicknamed 'Josh', is a 600-metre-long funnel that can be pulled across the ocean to collect any plastics that are floating on the surface. The Ocean Cleanup team uses data and modelling to steer the funnel towards the areas with most plastic.

SQUAWK!
Josh and his older sister Jenny (AKA System 02) have already removed thousands of kilograms of plastic waste from the oceans, and Josh is working hard even now to remove more.

THE GREAT PACIFIC GARBAGE PATCH

The Great Pacific Garbage Patch is the largest collection of ocean plastic on the planet, located in the Pacific Ocean between US states Hawaii and California. It's three times the size of France and scientists believe it contains about 1.8 trillion pieces of garbage – 250 pieces for every human in the world!

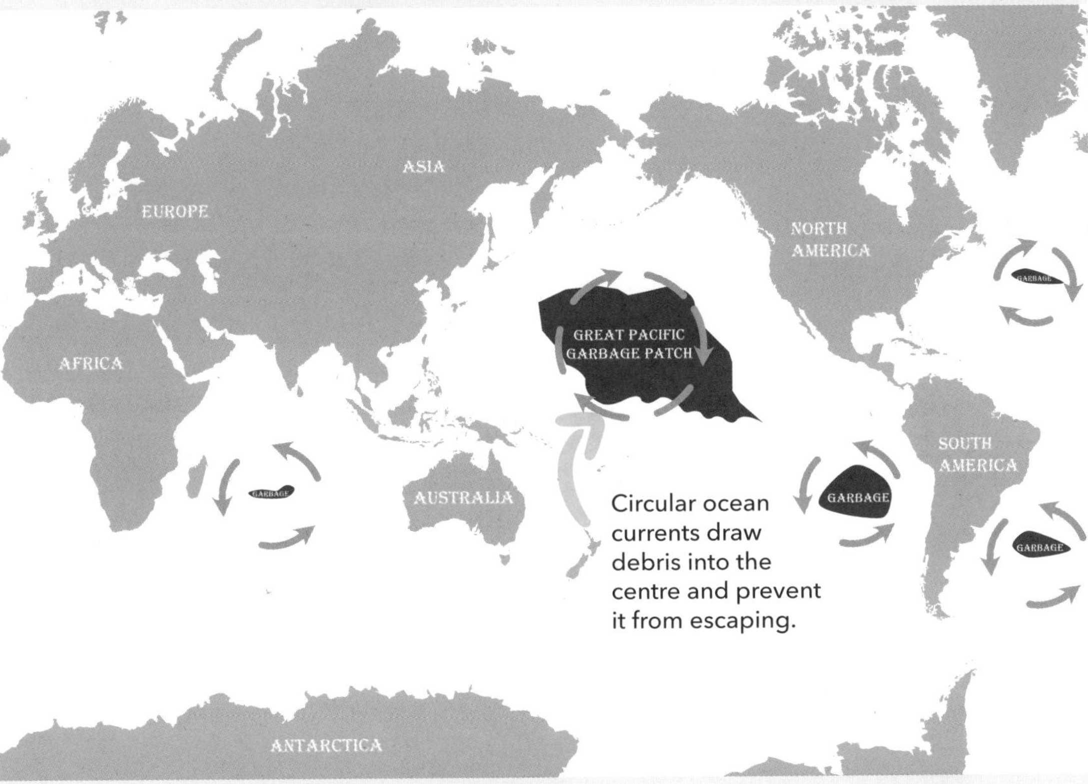

Plastic accumulates in this part of the ocean due to the system of circular ocean currents there – also called an ocean gyre.

While The Great Pacific Garbage Patch is the largest of its kind, there are also four other areas of ocean where this occurs (as shown above).

INTERCEPTING RIVER RUBBISH

To prevent any more plastic from reaching the oceans, The Ocean Cleanup team is installing interceptors in rivers, which act as barriers to block plastic from getting any further. The plastic can then be collected easily for recycling or disposal.

There are 3 million rivers in the world and The Ocean Cleanup team believes that just 1000 of those are responsible for about 80% of all the plastic pollution that flows into the oceans. So, they are aiming to install interceptors in all 1000 of these rivers.

WHAT HAPPENS TO ALL THAT PLASTIC?

In the words of The Ocean Cleanup's Recycling Manager John Verhoeven, 'there is no such thing as waste – only wasted resources'. With that mantra in mind, the group recycles the majority of the plastic it collects into durable new products that give the waste a new purpose, turning the problem into a solution. One example of this was The Ocean Cleanup Sunglasses, a one-off experiment to turn trash to treasure, and providing enough money to fund the clean-up of an area of the oceans that totalled half a million football fields in size.

Going forward, The Ocean Cleanup crew are working with partners to develop new products using the plastic they collect, such as for parts in electric vehicles, which helps to keep our oceans clean and those valuable materials in use.

> **“It is the worst of times but it is the best of times because we still have a chance.”**

Sylvia Earle, one of the first female oceanographers, speaking on plastic pollution.

THE GOOD NEWS
AUSSIE SCHOOLS TAKING ACTION

After reading about those big projects happening here in Australia and around the world, you might be wondering how you can play a part in tackling the huge plastic problem. Heaps of Australian school students have been wondering exactly the same thing, and many are already getting involved in the war on waste – and having a big impact!

STEPPING UP

Schools have always been an important part of Australia's action on plastic pollution. From what's going into the lunchbox to anti-litter campaigns and learning about recycling (and then teaching it at home!), students are key soldiers in the war on plastic. In 2018, the Australian Broadcasting Corporation (the ABC) first aired its *War on Waste* series. It partnered with Kiama High School and showed how it was possible to cut in half the amount of waste sent to landfill over just two school terms. Thanks to this successful initiative, more students and teachers around Australia have picked up the sustainability baton to run their own projects, helping to make the Australian school community both eco-aware and eco-friendly. The school reported a massive reduction in litter around the playground following the *War on Waste* program, showing how students took the initiative to heart and had a prolonged sense of pride and responsibility around their waste-reducing achievements.

REUSE IS KEY

After watching the *War on Waste* series, inspired students from North Adelaide Primary School set out on their own war on waste. They first looked into what waste the school was producing, and honed in on the biggest culprits as their first zone of attack, making coffee cups and plastic bags their first targets for elimination. To make it sustainable, the students started selling reusable coffee cups and calico bags at the school, and then went out into the community and asked local cafes to support their efforts by offering discounts to people who used them. The school also implemented a 'Nude food' day, where everyone's lunchboxes were free from throwaway packaging to cut down on their plastic footprint even more. Next initiative: compost bins for food scraps.

CLEAN-UP ROBOTS

At South Australia's Westminster School, students have made the most of the robotics program taught there to design robots that clean up rubbish from bodies of water. To try out their robot designs, the students created prototypes made from simple materials they found around their homes and school, and then powered and manoeuvred them using robotic technology – which the students wrote the code for themselves. These could be our future environmental engineers!

BANNING BINS

Melbourne Girls' College was also inspired by the ABC's *War on Waste* program. In 2019, the students there kicked off with a bin ban following a waste audit that found the school sent about 954 cubic metres of trash to landfill in 2018, which was not only costly to the environment, but also to the school, who footed a bill of $13,000. Since then, the school sustainability team has consulted with parents and students with the aim of teaching them to take responsibility for their rubbish while also encouraging families to purchase foods with less packaging. To encourage accountability, the school has also set up a token system, which rewards students who are consistently using reusable packaging with prizes.

Blue Planet

THE GOOD NEWS
THE TURTLE TRIBE

Teenager Ned Heaton has already done a huge amount to help the environment – starting at the age of just 11. That was when he set up a company called The Turtle Tribe as part of a passionate mission to help save the oceans from plastic pollution.

KID ON A MISSION

Ned and his family went camping each year on the beaches of Moreton Island. Unfortunately, the family found they were sharing the beach with as much plastic as wildlife, and so would spend days of their trips helping to pick up plastic from the sand. Eleven-year-old Ned returned to his home in Queensland passionate about bringing about change, and with the support of his parents and the guidance of two mentors from the Youth in Business program, Ned started his own business – The Turtle Tribe – to help fight the waste created by plastic toothbrushes.

THE TURTLE TRIBE

During his beach clean-ups, Ned found toothbrushes were a common culprit. He couldn't understand why something bought so regularly would be made of plastic – a material that doesn't break down. Ned discovered that bamboo was a great eco-friendly alternative material for toothbrushes – it grows easily and quickly, it's strong and it is biodegradable. With the help of his local dentist, Ned designed a bamboo toothbrush, and The Turtle Tribe is now one of the largest suppliers of bamboo toothbrushes in Australia.

> **SQUAWK!**
> Bamboo is actually a giant grass. Its roots are shallow and grow like lawn but its stems are woody, hard and strong – perfect for toothbrushes! Some bamboo varieties can grow up to a metre a day!

BEYOND THE TOOTHBRUSH

Ned's inspiring story has seen him win awards for his success as a business innovator and change maker. And he uses every bit of media coverage he gets to push his mission to ban plastic toothbrushes.

As well as selling bamboo toothbrushes, The Turtle Tribe sells other plastic-free, sustainable products, such as toothpaste tablets (replacing toothpaste in plastic tubes) and non-plastic dental floss made of silk or corn.

Ocean Crusaders, a not-for-profit company that is on a mission to clean up Australia's waterways, receives 10% of all of The Turtle Tribe's business profits. And Ned has also pledged to give away 1 million bamboo toothbrushes to help change people's buying habits to more sustainable options.

Ned is also committed to education, having spoken to thousands of school students about how they can make a change. He's even published a children's picture book to educate and inspire kids, using it to also launch a school education campaign empowering kids to help raise funds for their school by selling bamboo toothbrushes in their local community.

In 2022, Ned presented a petition to Queensland Minister for the Environment, Meaghan Scanlon, requesting the addition of plastic toothbrushes to the list of plastic-product bans.

Blue Planet

THE GOOD NEWS

CORAL BABIES

We hear a lot about how coral is being badly affected by climate change, but we don't hear as much about how coral might be restored to health. Thanks to the determination of a group of marine biologists on the Great Barrier Reef, a natural phenomenon has been given a helping hand by science to ensure old coral gets new life.

WHERE IT ALL BEGAN

On a spring evening in 1981, a small group of marine biology researchers, including a young Peter Harrison, were diving on the Great Barrier Reef and discovered something incredible. It looked like an underwater snowstorm, but it was in fact trillions of brightly coloured bundles containing coral eggs and sperm cells. This 'broadcast spawning' event had never been seen before, and it had a profound impact upon Peter Harrison . . .

Over the coming decades, Harrison studied the waters around Heron Island on the Great Barrier Reef, and learned how to use this spectacular natural event to help restore damaged reef systems. With other researchers at Southern Cross University, Harrison was a part of the innovative 2012 team who helped to effectively restore damaged coral reefs in the Phillipines, and, in 2016, started on the coral of the Great Barrier Reef.

HOW IT WORKS

Finely meshed nets are used to capture microscopic coral eggs and sperm that float to the surface of the water at different times of the year. The science team focus on the corals that have survived bleaching and can tolerate heat to give the new coral a better chance of surviving the continuing climate change. The team ensure the sex cells meet and place the new coral babies in protected floating enclosures to grow. When big enough, the team then release the baby corals back onto damaged reefs, seeding them into coral systems.

SUCCESS!

The Great Barrier Reef coral babies project was the first of its kind and a huge success. By 2021, 22 large coral groups planted by Harrison's team had grown to maturity and were themselves ready to give birth to even more coral. These new coral structures even continued growing during a bleaching event, showing that they may be resilient to some of the effects of climate change. In November 2021, the spectacular spawning event occurred, giving great hope that damaged parts of the Great Barrier Reef can be restored.

A HELPING HAND

A recent survey showed that the greatest coral bleaching on the Great Barrier Reef occurred in the parts that were most visited by tourists. We know the damage humans can do, and have done, to ecosystems, and so it's fantastic that humans can be part of coral's good news story, too. The Great Barrier Reef is currently losing breeding corals faster than most of them can regrow naturally, meaning this type of intervention may be essential to save the reef. Harrison hopes to offer this helping hand to reefs around the world in the future, and reverse at least some of the damage done by climate change.

SQUAWK!

The Great Barrier Reef is the largest reef in the world. It is 2,300km long, which is the same size as the entire states of Victoria and Tasmania put together! It is so big that astronauts can see it from the moon.

Blue Planet

THE GOOD NEWS
TURTLE TRACKERS

In the dead of night, on a protected island off the coast of Western Australia, park rangers and volunteers place tags on pregnant loggerhead turtles. They tag them so that they can track where they go as they swim through the oceans, and then help them and their babies survive.

To be a turtle tracker, you must be as quiet as a ninja and not afraid of the dark. When it's pitch-black outside, the trackers don head-torches and creep along the beach on the almost deserted Dirk Hartog Island. When they spot a pregnant turtle, the trackers silently watch her dig a hole in the sand and lay around 100 eggs. When she's finished, the trackers tag and measure her as she makes a beeline for the ocean using her mighty flippers to push her heavy body through the sand.

KEEPING WATCH

The tags send signals to satellites in space, which researchers use to track the journeys of loggerheads as they swim great distances across the ocean. Tagging and measuring the turtles helps researchers monitor their health and numbers, so they can check that enough babies are being born to stop them from becoming extinct.

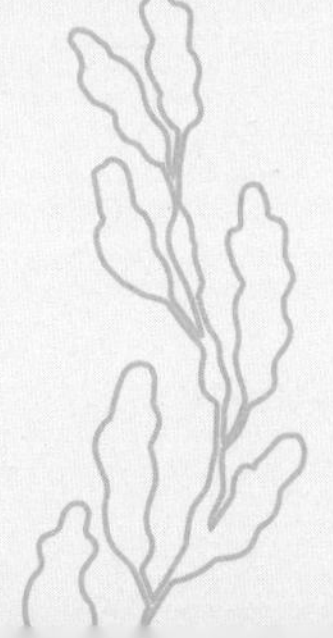

ABOUT THE LOGGERHEAD TURTLE

The world's biggest hard-shelled turtle species was named after the turtles' exceptionally large heads, which look a bit like a log and have powerful jaws to crush prey like crabs and clams – so be sure to keep your fingers safely away from them! Loggerheads are an endangered species, which means the number of loggerhead turtles in the world is very low. The turtles are under threat from habitat loss, pollution and human interference from things like fishing nets. Baby turtles are guided to the ocean by the light of the moon, so bright lights from human activity along the coast can also attract baby turtles inland, where they are more likely to die, instead of towards the ocean. If a loggerhead turtle manages to stay alive into adulthood, it can live for around 70 years.

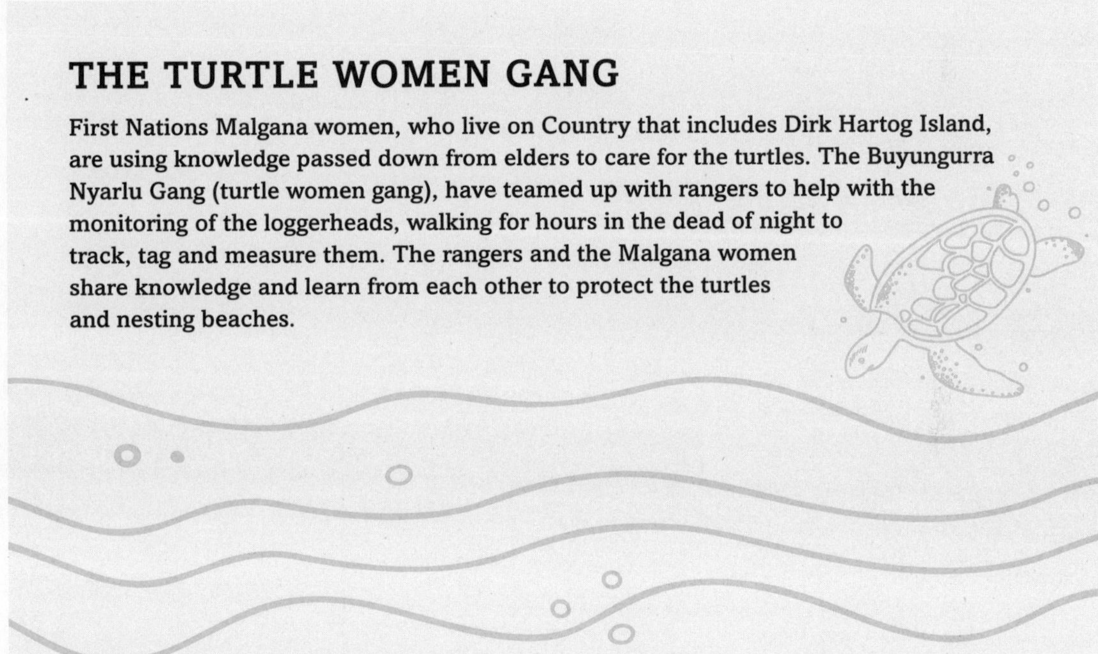

THE TURTLE WOMEN GANG

First Nations Malgana women, who live on Country that includes Dirk Hartog Island, are using knowledge passed down from elders to care for the turtles. The Buyungurra Nyarlu Gang (turtle women gang), have teamed up with rangers to help with the monitoring of the loggerheads, walking for hours in the dead of night to track, tag and measure them. The rangers and the Malgana women share knowledge and learn from each other to protect the turtles and nesting beaches.

SPECIAL POWERS

Loggerhead turtles are biofluorescent, which means they soak up sunlight during the day and then radiate it out as a different colour when it's dark, glowing a bright green. Scientists aren't sure what the turtles use this neat trick for, but some think it is a form of camouflage against other fluorescent creatures in the ocean, like coral, while others say it might be a way of communicating with each other. Either way, it makes the loggerhead turtle an extremely special species that needs our protection from becoming extinct.

The Power of Nature

THE POWER OF NATURE

Nature is the collective term for the physical world around us. It is the landscape of Earth itself, it is plant and animal life on Earth and it is the natural systems that make the world go round. Nature can be powerful or gentle – the term 'force of nature' is one of strength, while 'Mother Nature' relates to its nurturing and life-creating qualities. We benefit from Nature in many ways. More and more, humans are looking to natural products rather than human-made, and to spend time in Nature to holiday and regenerate. However, human activities and presence often have a negative impact on the very thing we seek out. In this chapter, we look at the power of Nature to regenerate both itself and us, as well as what we can do to help it thrive. (Spoiler alert: the answer is often to let it be!)

NATURE'S CYCLES

Nature has developed complex cycles that keep the world in order and alive by renewing itself. All of Nature's cycles are based on the same principle: balance. When Nature is in charge, there isn't too much or too little of anything and, most importantly, there is no waste. Nature has developed this self-sufficient and harmonious way of making sure everything is valued and sustained.

There are five main cycles in Nature:

- Water cycle (see page 17)
- Rock cycle (see page 43)
- Oxygen cycle (see page 44)
- Carbon cycle (see page 45)
- Nitrogen cycle (see page 46)

THE ROCK CYCLE

There are three types of rocks – igneous, sedimentary and metamorphic. The rocks we see around us on the surface are mostly igneous rocks. Sedimentary and metamorphic rocks are usually underground. In the rock cycle, rocks change from one form to another. It takes millions of years for rocks to complete the full cycle.

1. Weathering and erosion break apart igneous rocks from Earth's surface.

2. Igneous rocks are transported by wind and water to the ocean, where they are deposited.

3. Further erosion during transportation breaks down igneous rocks into tiny grains, called sediment, which settles on the ocean floor.

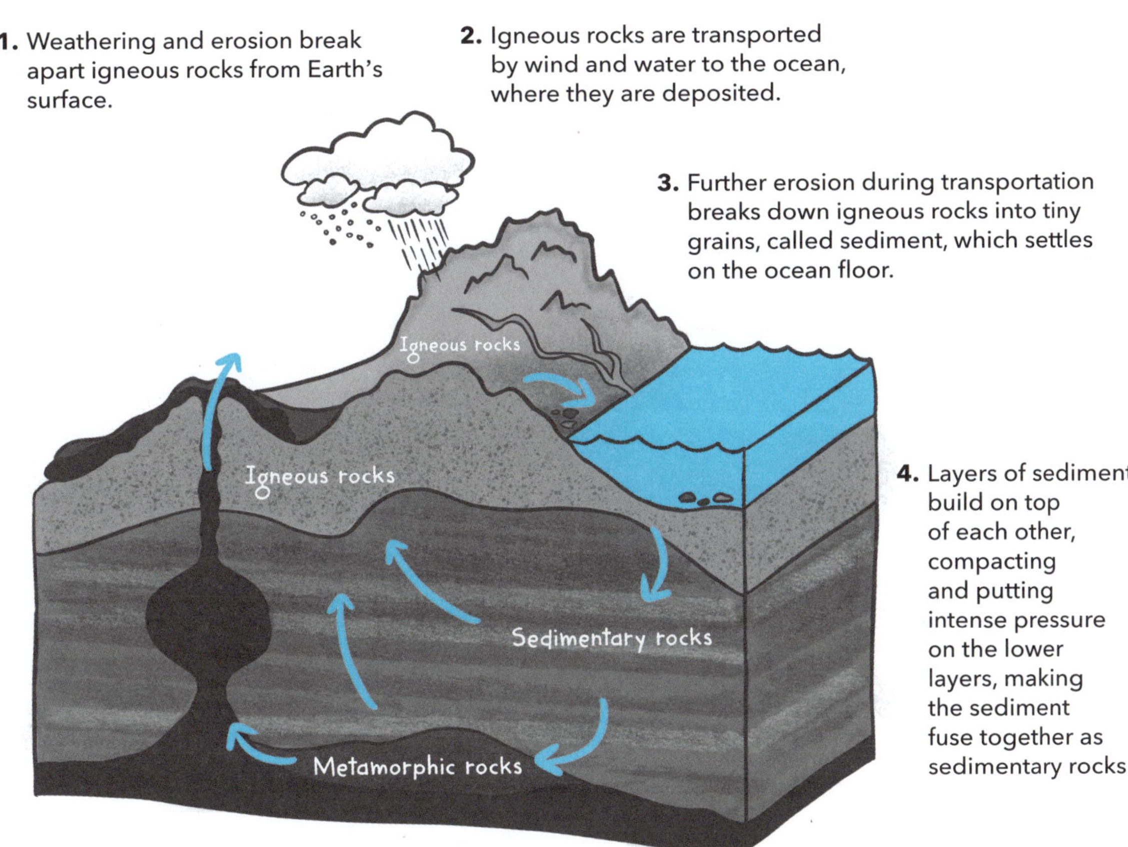

4. Layers of sediment build on top of each other, compacting and putting intense pressure on the lower layers, making the sediment fuse together as sedimentary rocks.

5. Some sedimentary rocks make their way to the surface to start the breaking-down process again. Other sedimentary rocks move deeper underground where intense heat and pressure change them into metamorphic rocks.

6. Some metamorphic rocks make their way to the surface to start the breaking-down process again. Hotter temperatures melt some metamorphic rocks into liquid magma.

7. Magma rises through the layers of rocks. Sometimes it cools and crystallises back into igneous rocks. Other times it erupts out of the ground as lava and cools on Earth's surface, changing back into igneous rocks.

THE OXYGEN CYCLE

About one-fifth of Earth's atmosphere is oxygen, most of which exists close to the ground in the air we breathe. So it's no coincidence that most life on Earth lives at ground level, since all animals, humans included, need oxygen. As with everything that Nature does, the oxygen cycle ensures a balance that maintains life on Earth.

21% oxygen

1% other gases, including carbon

78% nitrogen

SQUAWK!

Carbon (C) in our bodies combines with the oxygen (O_2) we breath in to create carbon dioxide (CO_2).

1. All animals breathe in oxygen, which our bodies absorb to help fuel them.

2. Animals then breathe out carbon dioxide in a process called respiration.

3. During the day, plants absorb this carbon dioxide and release oxygen in a process called photosynthesis.

4. The sun powers photosynthesis in plants to help them convert water and carbon dioxide into food to help them grow. They release oxygen during this process.

DID YOU KNOW?

Oxygen levels in the air decrease the higher you go. If a human climbs to 8000 metres above sea level or higher, there is not enough oxygen to keep them alive. That is why mountain climbers call it the Death Zone.

THE CARBON CYCLE

Carbon is in every living thing on the planet and moves between these living organisms and other parts of Nature like the air, soil and our oceans. But carbon, including carbon dioxide (often written as CO2), is constantly moving in a complex cycle that connects all of Nature, with some natural processes taking carbon out of the atmosphere and some putting it back in. Nature does a great job of balancing carbon in this cycle, to make sure there is just enough carbon in the atmosphere to keep Earth warm enough for life to survive.

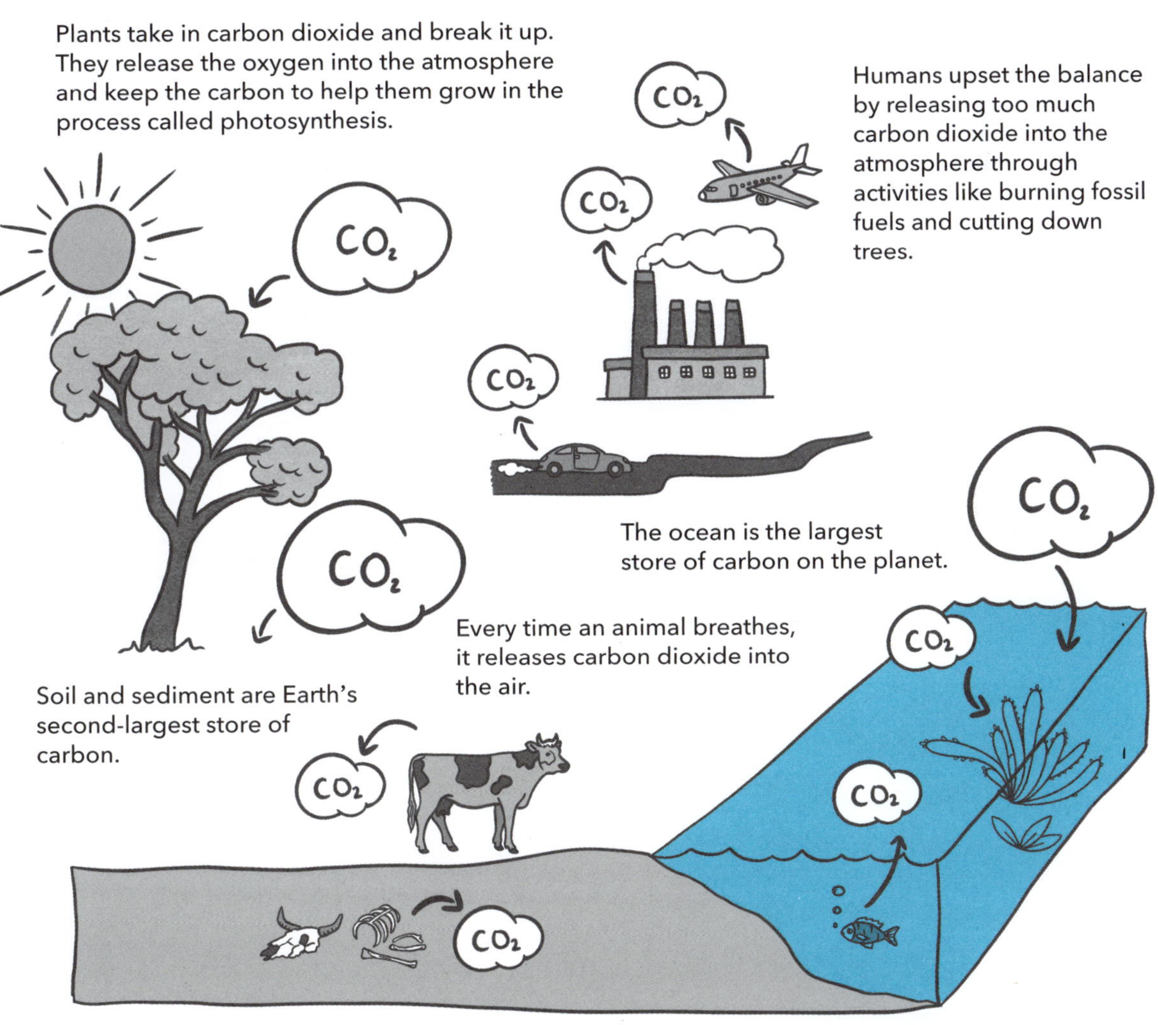

When living things die, they decay and release carbon in the process. Some is released into the atmosphere where it bonds again with oxygen to form carbon dioxide; some carbon becomes fossil fuels that are stored in the ground.

Fish also release carbon dioxide when they breathe, and ocean plants take in carbon and release oxygen in the same way as those on land do.

THE NITROGEN CYCLE

Nitrogen is another element that is essential for a healthy world. It moves through the air, soil and living things in a never-ending cycle. Nitrogen is a gas that makes up about 78% of the air we breathe. But living things can't use the nitrogen in air – we simply breathe it out again, unchanged. To be useful, nitrogen needs to be changed into nitrate.

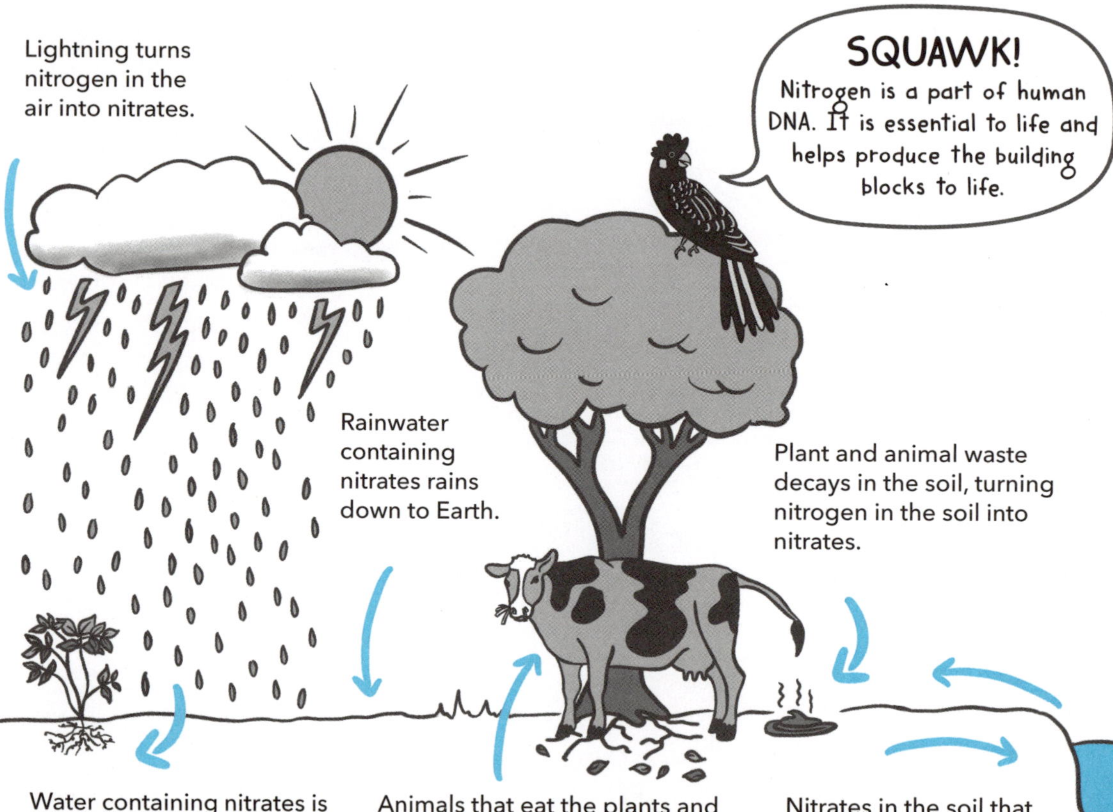

DID YOU KNOW?

Nitrate is nitrogen fused with oxygen – similar to how carbon dioxide is carbon fused with oxygen. Nitrate is highly soluble and so is often found in water such as in rain following lightning, and in groundwater.

> **Nature is a self-regulating system, in which everything is in a constant state of flux and change, always moving in cycles.**
>
> David Suzuki, scientist, author and environmental activist

LIVING IN A GREENHOUSE

When carbon and oxygen bond together, they become carbon dioxide. Carbon dioxide is a greenhouse gas that traps heat in the atmosphere, making it important in keeping our world the right temperature for us and other animals and plants to live in. The problem is that if there is too much carbon dioxide (and other greenhouse gases), the world gets too hot. That is why many people are trying to reduce the amount of carbon dioxide and other greenhouse gases that human activities produce. (For more on the effect of greenhouse gases, see page 18.)

EARTH'S EARTH

Soil is more than just dirt. It is the foundation of all life on Earth. It is a part of every cycle of Nature. It is filled with nutrients to support plant growth. It recycles dead plants and animals into nutrients that feed new plants. It filters our water and air. It stores large quantities of elements such as carbon to keep the balance in Nature just right. And it is also home to many essential organisms, from microscopic bacteria to creepy crawlies. It's no wonder we named earth after Planet Earth.

All soil is made up of four things: finely ground rock, water, air and humus, which is decomposed plant and animal matter, also called organic matter. The different types of soil that you find beneath your feet have different mixes of the four elements listed above, and are known as 'fine earth'. Which type of soil is found in a particular spot on Earth depends on many factors including climate, wildlife and the type of parent rock that the finely ground rock is made from.

Loamy soil (sometimes called silt) is a well-balanced soil, made up of a mix of finely ground rocks that includes coarse sand, tiny silt and sticky clay. Many different types of plants and animals thrive in and on loamy soil because it allows plant roots to grow easily and water to drain from it while still maintaining a healthy level of moisture.

Clay soil is sticky when wet and cracked when dry. It is made up of the tiniest soil particles and holds onto water without letting it drain. It therefore becomes easily waterlogged.

Sandy soil contains more air than water, and the particles that make it up are dry and light. Water drains straight through it very easily.

DIFFERENT LAYERS OF SOIL

Soil has many different layers, which scientists call horizons. Each horizon has distinct features. The horizon sizes vary across the different soil-types. The diagram here shows the relative horizon sizes for a loamy soil.

Organic horizon is the part of the soil that we see on Earth's surface. It is mainly made up of humus - dead plant parts that are slowly decomposing.

Topsoil is a plant's happy place. It has lots of nutrients for plants to feed on and grow, and has lots of tiny air holes for their roots to grow into easily.

Subsoil is more compacted than topsoil, with less air holes and less nutrients.

Parent material is what the soil above it is mostly made up of. It is parts of the bedrock that have been broken apart by erosion and plant activity.

Bedrock is the deepest part of soil and is what all earth sits on top of.

SQUAWK!

There are more living organisms in one handful of soil than there are people on the planet. Soil is made up of billions of tiny bacteria, fungi, and other microorganisms.

WHY IS SOIL SO IMPORTANT TO HUMANS?

All plant life relies on soil to grow, and so it follows that humans rely on soil to grow crops for food. Without healthy soil and the nutrients it contains, humans would struggle to feed everyone. Soil also acts as an effective water filter and supplies us with lifesaving antibiotics. It is literally the foundation upon which we build our homes and cities. And, soil is one of Earth's biggest stores of carbon – land plants and soils hold about 2,500 gigatonnes of carbon, which is three times more than the amount of carbon in the atmosphere, making it super-important in combating the climate crisis.

WHERE DO PLANTS STORE CARBON?

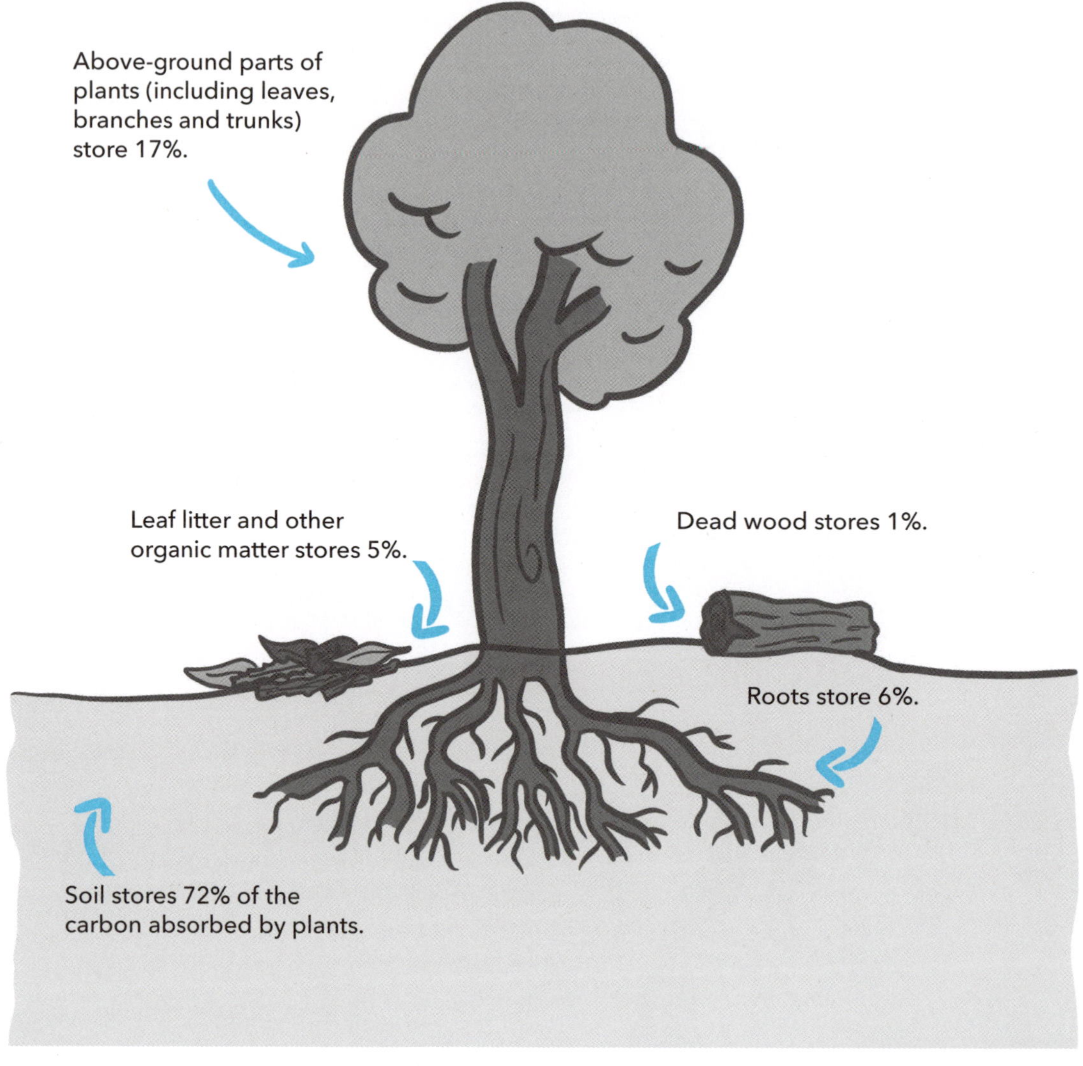

WHAT ARE WE DOING TO OUR SOIL?

We need healthy, fertile soil for so many reasons, and yet many of our activities are affecting soil quality and its ability to fulfill those vital balancing roles. New soil takes hundreds of years to be made, so it is important to protect it.

Waste production

Where there are humans there is waste, most of which is harmful to the environment and is buried in the ground in what we call landfill. As the buried garbage degrades, it releases harmful greenhouse gases (20% of methane emissions come from landfill) and contaminates soil and water in the area.

Agricultural practices

Excessive farming of land (such as grazing, crop growing and use of fertilisers and pesticides) drains the soil of nutrients and humus so plants can no longer grow there. Over the past 150 years, half of the world's nutrient-rich topsoil has been depleted.

Infrastructure development

Land and soil that has been concreted over by humans is unable to filter water, and so water runs over it directly into waterways such as streams and rivers, taking our pollution with it.

Air pollution

Polluted particles from emissions of factories, cars, planes and many other sources eventually fall to Earth and contaminate the soil and water, which can kill plants.

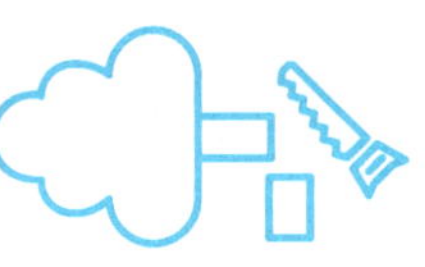

Deforestation

Cutting down trees exposes soil to excessive weathering and erosion, which degrades it of the nutrients needed for plants to grow and leaves it vulnerable to removal by wind and rain. The drastic change in soil composition also reduces the amount of carbon the soil can store.

Human population growth

As the human population grows, towns and cities become bigger, literally paving over Nature. People also move around the world, and throughout history have taken elements of their natural environment with them, damaging the balance of the native vegetation in the country they move to. These invasive species take the nutrition in the soil away from native species. Because Australia has a unique natural environment, governments have created very strict biosecurity laws so people can't bring in other plant and animal species that could potentially threaten the fragile balance.

Climate change

Human-induced global warming is causing the frozen carbon-rich soils known as permafrost in the Arctic to melt, releasing thousands of years of frozen carbon into the atmosphere. This is then accelerating climate change, as the amount of carbon in the atmosphere continues to grow and causes warmer temperatures.

THE GOOD NEWS
NATURAL FARMING

In most modern farming practices, the goal is to get high yields of crops from the soil. And the introduction of nitrate fertilisers in the early 20th century succeeded in tripling world food production from the same amount of land in the space of 40 years. However, we now know that nitrate fertilisers harm the environment in many ways. So, what's the solution in a world with limited farmland and an ever-increasing human population that relies on farming to feed it?

REGENERATIVE FARMING

Many farmers are now looking to Nature for ways to farm and look after soil that are kinder to the environment. Sam Vincent, a self-confessed reluctant farmer, became inspired by his father's drive to replenish the nutrient-poor soil on their farm in the Yass Valley, NSW. He quit his job as a journalist in Canberra and joined his father's efforts, now working full time as a cattle and fig farmer. Opposite are some of the methods they're using.

COMPOST EVERYTHING

This not only reduces physical waste, but also creates a natural fertiliser that ensures no part of Nature's cycle has been wasted.

IMPROVING THE SOIL

The reason chemical fertilisers are nitrate-based is because the nitrogen that's essential for growth is the most depleted nutrient in soil once crops have been harvested. In regenerative farming, a 'cover crop' is planted after a harvest to help the soil regenerate. Cover crops like legumes and clover are excellent at replenishing soil's nitrogen levels. Other cover crops might have deep roots to help keep the soil in place to reduce soil erosion, thick foliage that blocks sunlight from reaching the soil to prevent weeds from germinating, or attract animals that naturally take care of crop-loving pests.

IMPROVING THE FUNCTION OF CREEKS

By planting native grasses around and at the start of a creek, the water that flows into it is essentially filtered and cleaned. Installing troughs for livestock to drink from also helps to maintain the water quality in the creek as well as protecting the vegetation around it, which will then attract wildlife – a key sign of water quality. As we know, soil that is healthy holds on to more water, which is important for times of drought.

ROTATIONAL GRAZING

Regenerative grazing of livestock such as cattle and sheep is a way of better managing their effect on the land so that grazing actually gives back to the soil that produces the feed. By dividing a large paddock into smaller ones and then moving (rotating) the animals between them, the land has a chance to recover from any grazing using the natural fertiliser (nutrient-rich manure) left by the animals.

NO-TILL FARMING

Turning the earth before planting seeds is known as tilling, and is common in modern farming practices. It makes it quick and easy to plant new crops, but leaves the soil bare, making it more vulnerable to soil erosion. It also destroys the intricate web of a healthy soil's make-up, which includes the holes created by hard-working worms, the structure formed by root systems as well as bacteria and organisms living in the soil. No-till farming can maintain the natural health of soil by letting it be, improving its structure which makes it better at absorbing and filtering water and, in turn, can lead to higher yields of crops. Healthy soil is also key to storing problematic excess carbon.

PLANTING A LOT OF TREES

Trees provide wind protection and shade as well as attracting insect pollinators and wildlife that acts as a natural pest control. They also help soil structure with their root systems and increase soil health thanks to the leaf litter they drop, which adds to the soil's nutrient count.

After 40 years, the Vincent family's regenerative farming efforts are clearly visible. Not just in productivity and profitability, but in the whole environment on which they farm and live, which has seen a renewed biodiverse community flourish. And other regenerative farmers are seeing the same results. This farming method is pioneering because it focuses just as much on giving back to the soil as it does on taking from it.

WIDER IMPLICATIONS

Healthy soil is key to a balanced environment, producing food rich in vitamins that makes for healthy humans. Fruits and vegetables are full of vitamins that help you to grow and fight disease, and we now know that food grown using less invasive farming methods can contain a higher percentage of vitamins than food grown using ploughed fields and chemical fertiliser.

> "Food is only as healthy as the soil in which it is grown."
>
> **Anna Gibson, soil conservationist**

CREATING A GIANT SOIL CATALOGUE

Data about soil is so important that millions of dollars are being spent in Australia to set up a soil data system. This will help create a standardised way of collecting information about the make-up of soil across Australia, and will be an important resource for farmers and scientists to help them manage land health.

ECO TIP

You can help create soil that's rich in organic matter and reduce waste going to landfill by starting your own composting bin or worm farm. If you don't have space for one at home, check out your local community or school garden.

THE GOOD NEWS

SEED BANKS

Everyone knows it is a good idea to save money, probably in a bank, but not everyone knows the importance of saving seeds, too. Around 1700 seed banks exist around the world for this very purpose. They are special storage units for seeds and plant cuttings – a bit like a savings account for the natural world, set up by humans to ensure that in the future we don't run out of food or the medicine that plants can provide.

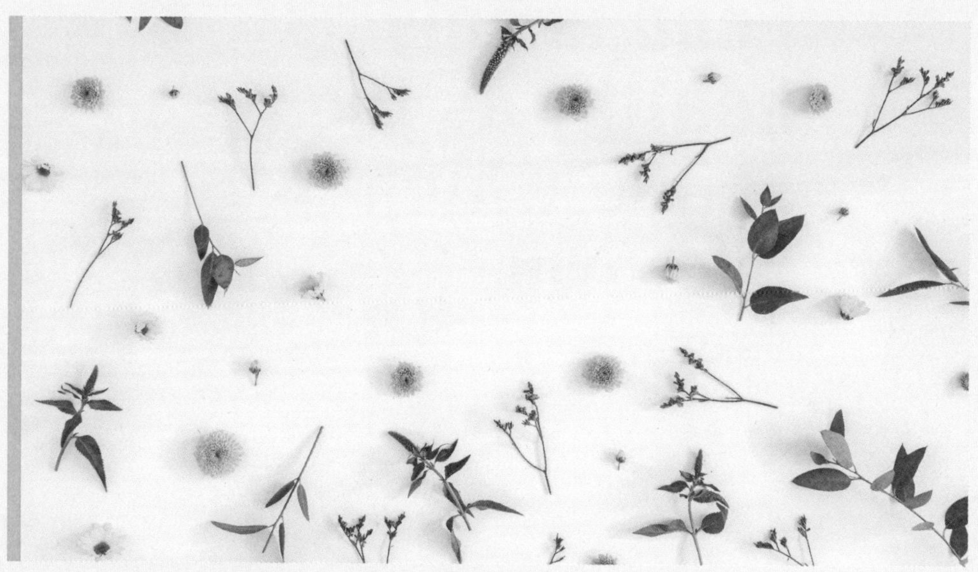

WHY ARE SEED BANKS IMPORTANT?

We rely on plants for most of our basic needs including food, medicine, clothing, shelter, clean air and water. But with an estimated two-fifths of plant species around the world at risk of extinction, seed banks are an insurance policy for our future.

Humans tend to focus on growing the crops and plants that we already know we can use, reducing the variety of vegetation across the world with activities such as clearing native bushlands to make way for farms.

In the natural world, plants have changed and adapted over millions of years of evolution, and so it is imperative we safeguard that knowledge and variation in our seeds in case of natural or human disaster. The collectors and researchers who manage the seed banks hope to ensure diverse crops and vegetation remain a part of our world, widening our potential for different food crops as well as storing the wild relatives of our priority crops.

THE WORLD'S COLDEST SEED BANK

The Svalbard Global Seed Vault has a couple of pet names including The Doomsday Vault and the Noah's Ark of Seeds. It is a global seed bank located deep in the snow on a frozen island in the Arctic Circle. The location in Norway was specifically chosen in case the vault's refrigeration system ever fails, in the hope that surrounding permafrost will conserve the seeds. If a global catastrophe hit, this seed vault would allow humans to regrow the crops needed for survival. The bank has space for 2.25 billion individual seeds.

SAVING THE DINOSAUR TREE

The Wollemi pine is one of the world's rarest and most threatened tree species. It is a unique plant native to Australia, with bark looking like bubbling chocolate and up to 20 trunks for one tree. A single Wollemi pine can live for thousands of years because the trees reproduce by cloning themselves. The pine tree was thought to be extinct until a grove of around 100 of the trees was discovered in 1994 within the Greater Blue Mountains World Heritage area of NSW. To protect them from human interference, their location is kept secret from the public, and to ensure these pines are not lost to the world again, seeds have been banked and cuttings taken. Hundreds of these cuttings have been planted in other special locations as insurance populations. They are now also available to plant at home!

During the Black Summer fires of 2019, firefighters put water in the soil around the grove and dropped substances from helicopters to slow down the fires. Their fearless efforts stopped the fires from burning through the last remaining old-growth Wollemi pines.

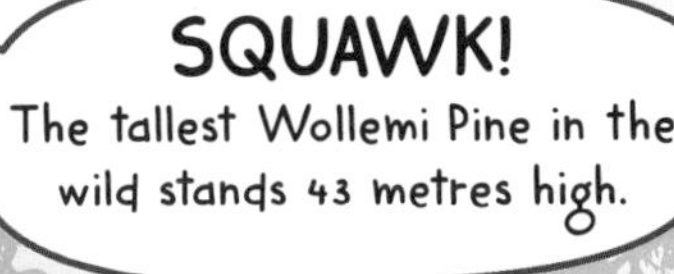

THE GOOD NEWS
STAND UP FOR THE TREES

Trees can't stand up against chainsaws and bulldozers. And so it's up to us to do it for them. One group of determined people in Western Australia have campaigned for decades to protect trees from logging in the state's native forests . . .

THE GOOD FIGHT

Western Australians have been protesting for more than a century against the destruction of their forests due to industry activity such as mining and logging. The native old-growth forests in southwest WA have been the focus of these protests, as they contain timber giants that don't grow anywhere else in the world – huge stands of tingle, jarrah, karri, marri, tuart and wandoo trees. Through tireless protests and campaigns to raise public awareness, environmental activist groups have become a strong force to be reckoned with over recent decades. As a result of public pressure, logging has now stopped and 400,000 hectares of unique native WA forest will be protected. The ultimate goal is full protection of WA's native forests and woodlands from logging and clearing.

WHY DO WE CUT DOWN TREES?

People have been cutting down trees for many different reasons for thousands of years. Sometimes it was to use the wood for fuel, or to make things like buildings, furniture and paper. Sometimes it was to clear the fertile land for farming or for mining. Since colonisation, Australia has lost an estimated 40% of its forests, which mainly exist in coastal areas where the soils are more fertile and the climate less harsh – it's no coincidence that these are the areas where Australia's settlers chose to live. But now that we understand the cost of cutting down aging forests, it's important to protect those that are left, ensuring native plant species and ecosystems are not lost to history. Once they are gone, they cannot be replaced.

WA Forest Alliance.

≡ MORE GOOD NEWS ≡

With the loss of so much old-growth forest, some savvy WA residents are installing artificial hollows called 'cockatubes', which have been specifically made from recycled materials for the endangered Carnaby's black cockatoo.

A Carnaby's black cockatoo in an artificial hollow built by Wally Kerkhof.

A COSY HOME

The reason old-growth forests are home to so much life is due to the fact that the trees are old and so have mature-tree features, such as hollows and holes, fallen logs, dead wood and shed bark – all of which provide homes for animals, and materials for nesting, food and soil nutrition. Tree hollows are especially important for many of Australia's animals, with about 40% of mammals and 20% of birds depending on hollows for roosting and nesting. Only mature trees have valuable hollows, and some wildlife will renovate a hollow to their liking using their beaks, teeth or claws.

SQUAWK!

The red tingle is one of the tallest trees in WA. One 400-year-old tree has been named Grandma Tingle due to the gnarly bark that has formed the shape of a face.

The Grandma Tingle tree.

THE GOOD NEWS
SELF-HEALING FORESTS

Tropical rainforests are among the world's best tools for fighting climate change. They store huge amounts of carbon, provide habitats for thousands of plants and animals and are home to many Indigenous peoples who both sustain them and rely on them.

WHAT ARE TROPICAL RAINFORESTS?

Tropical rainforests only exist in Earth's tropical zone, which runs around the centre of the globe – around the equator and between the Tropic of Cancer and Tropic of Capricorn. The tropical zone has both high temperatures and rainfall, which means it receives a lot of heat, water and light – the perfect conditions for plants to grow. Rainforests are particularly special because they have more species of trees than any other type of forest and, despite covering less than 10% of Earth's surface, they are home to more than half of the planet's biodiversity.

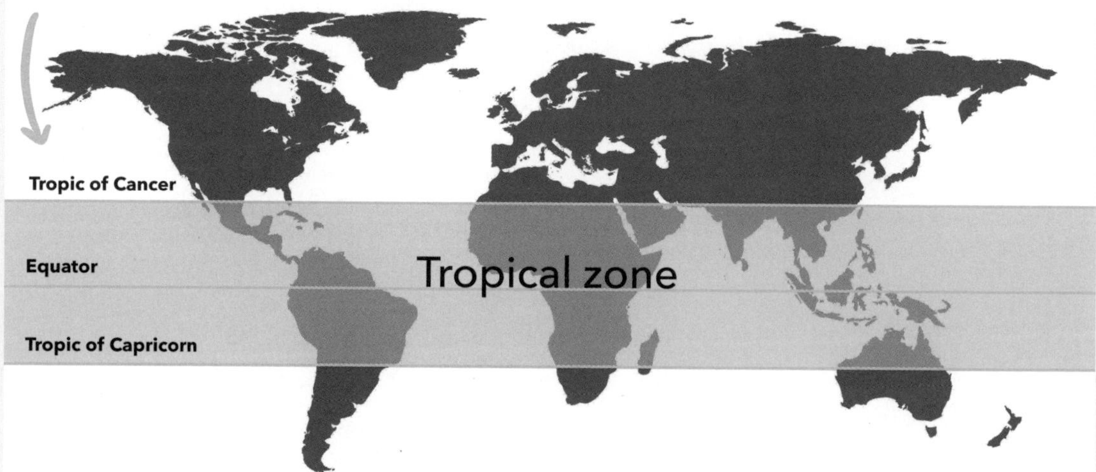

WHY ARE TROPICAL RAINFORESTS IN DANGER?

Many food and medicine products come from tropical-rainforest plants. Avocados, coconuts, bananas, spices and life-saving medicines are just some of the many things that humans rely on rainforests for. Unfortunately, to grow these fruits in large quantities for sale, some rainforests are cut down and farms are planted instead.

NATURE HELPING ITSELF

While many individuals and organisations are working together to prevent the destruction of rainforests from human activity and help restore them, many rainforests are finding ways to help themselves. In fact, it is becoming clear that forests which are left to their own devices have much better regrowth than those replanted by humans. These natural regrowth areas of rainforest, called secondary forests, are an effective way to restore the local and native ecosystem and wildlife, as well as help to slow down climate change.

DAINTREE REGROWTH

Husband and wife team Dave and Connie Pinson started the project Daintree Life as a way to showcase the Daintree region in far-north Queensland. Now they are on a mission to plant 500,000 trees in the 180-million-year-old Daintree Rainforest by 2030 to help preserve this unique region. Taking note of the evidence that points to rainforests helping themselves to become more fruitful, they are allowing the rainforest to regrow and heal naturally in areas where it's possible, and then planting to connect old growth forest with wildlife corridors.

ECO TIP

Planet Ark's Seedling Bank supplies native seedlings to community groups to plant where they're most needed. You can help by joining a school or community group on National Tree Day in July each year or raise funds for the Seedling Bank. Go to: treeday.planetark.org

SQUAWK!

In the moist rainforests of South and Central America, sloths move so slowly that algae and fungi grow on their fur. This makes the sloths' fur green and helps them blend in with the trees.

THE GOOD NEWS
A HOLE LOT OF HELP

Nature is clever. It knows how to look after itself, and it develops its own solutions to problems. Billions of years of changes on our planet have meant that Nature has adapted and evolved to maintain its precious balance. Since European settlement in Australia and the introduction of agriculture, Australian soils in many areas have been depleted of key nutrients and left very unhealthy. The soil horizons have been mixed up, soil has been compacted, carbon has been lost and organic matter (humus) has decreased.

But what colonial humans have ruined, Australia's unique Nature is doing some work to repair. Thanks to the dutiful digging of bandicoots and echidnas as they forage for food and build burrows, they create holes in the earth that not only help the soil health by turning over the soil and letting in moisture, but that could also be a key in tackling the climate crisis.

The holes they dig can be up to 50 centimetres wide and 15 centimetres deep – an impressive feat for these small critters – into which leaves, branches and other organic matter falls. Over time, this helps in many ways:

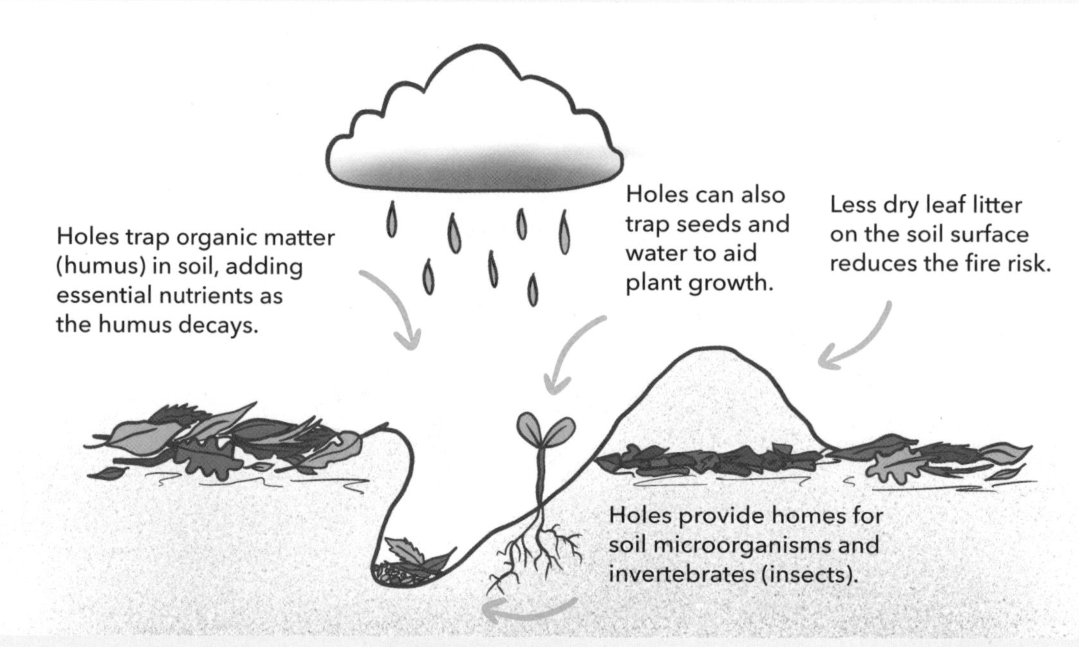

THE BIGGEST EARTHWORMS IN THE WORLD

Earthworms are another animal that help to improve the quality of soil. The dead plant matter they feed on enriches their poos with nutrients – especially the all-important nitrogen – which plants benefit from. Worm poo also helps the essential topsoil to stick together so that it isn't blown away. The never-ending tunnelling by worms through the soil loosens it to create more air holes and a better filter for water. Scientists have seen a direct link between the number of earthworms in soil and the health of its plant growth. And that's just your standard earthworm. Imagine the impact the Giant Gippsland earthworm has on the grasslands of Gippsland in Victoria. It's the longest earthworm in the world, growing up to 2 metres long! Researchers have reported loud gurgling sounds that the worms make underground – it's hard, noisy work down there.

THE GOOD NEWS
PLANT POWER

When you ride on the bus or drive in the car, your journey will be powered by fossil fuels (fuels made from fossils), such as oil, gas and coal. Even electric cars are mostly powered by fossil fuels in Australia because coal is still the main fuel we use to create electricity. Unfortunately, when humans use these fossil fuels, they pollute the air and contribute to climate change. Scientists around the world are looking for greener ways to fuel our world, and one secret ingredient might be in plants.

Sun's energy is absorbed by plants.

Oil rigs extract oil from deep in the ground.

Dead plants and animals decompose and are squashed beneath layers of rock where Earth's heat transforms them.

Coal is extracted for use in power stations to create electricity.

Gas is used for heating and cooking.

Oil is used in petrol-powered engines, such as cars.

WHAT ARE FOSSIL FUELS?

Fossil fuels are made from ancient plants and animals buried deep in the Earth. They take millions of years to form and there's only a limited amount of them, meaning the world's supply will eventually run out. When fossil fuels are burned to release their energy, they also release the million-year-old carbon they were storing as carbon dioxide – one of the greenhouse gases that is fuelling global warming.

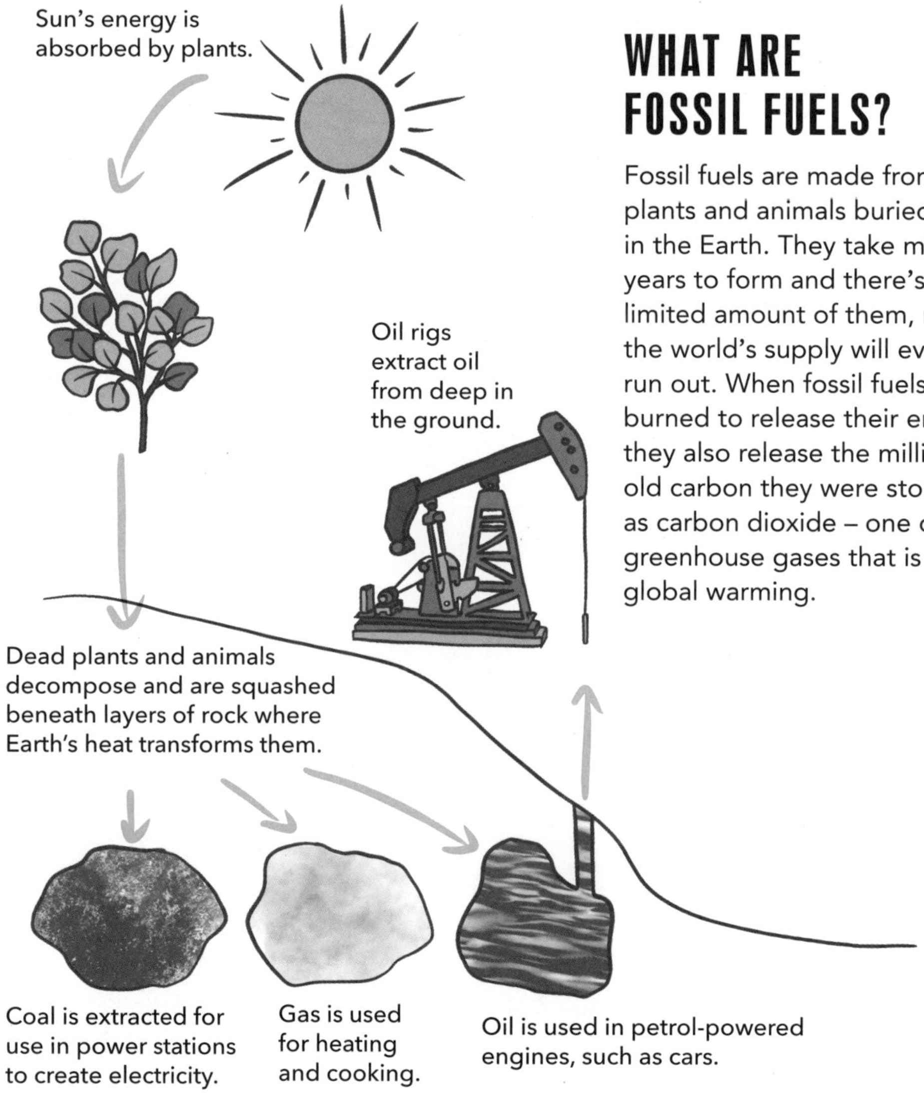

NATURE'S HIGHWAY

Scientists have been searching for new ways to fuel our world, and one of their solutions uses plants. Plant fuel is made from living plants so doesn't require waiting millions of years for natural processes to change them into fossils. It is a type of biofuel, made from biological (natural) materials. All biofuels are renewable; they will not run out. For plant-based biofuels, we can simply keep growing the plants as long as we need the fuel. And in using these fuels, we only release the carbon the plants use to grow rather than all the million-year-old stored carbon released by burning fossil fuels.

BEAUTY AND THE FRUIT

The Australian native Beauty Leaf Tree produces lots of oily fruits, and the oil from those fruits can be used as a fuel. The beauty of the Beauty Leaf Tree is that it can grow in poor-quality soil that is low in nutrients, and can still produce fruits in hot and dry conditions, as well as on waterlogged land – all of the conditions that most plants hate. This could be a game changer for the Australian biofuel industry, which has previously had to compete with farmers for the fertile, nutrient-rich land in places of favourable weather. The Beauty Leaf Tree could be the answer, with vast areas of available land in northern Australia's harsh climate.

MORE GOOD NEWS

Common crops grown on farms can also be turned into biofuels. These include sugar cane, corn, soybeans and canola. In the best-case scenario, parts of these plants that aren't eaten, such as stems or other off-cuts, are used in this process.

FUELLING OUR FUTURE

In 2022, Australia's government released a report called the Bioenergy Roadmap, which outlined their commitment to supporting new fuel sources in the future, one of which is a biofuel option. But a different fuel source isn't the only part of the puzzle; new vehicles and machines will need to be designed to run off those new biofuels. Now is the time for scientists and engineers of the future to get creative.

The Human Cycle

THE HUMAN CYCLE

In Nature's circle of life, there is no waste: everything is converted into a new form to be used again and again in a never-ending cycle. Unfortunately, the way we have constructed human life today means there is lots of waste. Humans have quite literally broken the cycle. But thankfully we are learning from our mistakes and starting to turn things around by following Nature's lead to make everything a circle.

THE HUMAN NON-CYCLE

Humans have always been excellent at using Earth's resources to make life more comfortable. From our early ancestors using wood and stone for fuel and shelter, to high-tech geniuses turning silicon into a computer chip, humans are very good at using raw materials to make something new. And with an ever-increasing population, our demand for more of everything is out of control.

FOOT ON THE GAS

The Industrial Revolution was a time in the 18th century when the human relationship with Nature and its resources changed forever. Before that point, only windmills and waterwheels used the power of Nature to do work for humans, such as in driving mills. But the discovery of fossil fuels and the energy they produce when they are burned led to the invention of the engine, which transformed human life beyond measure.

TAKING OVER THE WORLD

As industrialisation improved people's living standards, less people died from disease and more people lived longer lives, which led to a huge growth in the population. The world population has continued to explode as new innovations have led to ever-better standards of living. Today, there are more than 8 billion people around the globe.

WHO PAYS?

The huge number of humans has a massive impact on Earth's resources, especially when we take more than we need and throw away so much as waste. Nature pays the cost of our way of life, with depleted resources, damaged ecosystems, pollution and climate change. And what's the common culprit in all of these problems? Waste. Our societies that rule the modern world take, make and waste. This is called a linear economy.

A BROKEN CYCLE

Before humans took over the world, there was no such thing as waste. Everything on Earth was reused and recycled in a never-ending cycle that kept everything in balance and sustained life. In our current linear economy, many valuable materials and resources are being sent to landfill, breaking the natural cycle of returning these resources to Nature. By wasting these natural resources, we cause a range of problems from plastic litter that impacts wildlife to the release of greenhouse gases, which is upsetting the balance of our atmosphere and causing climate change. Discarding used materials and resources also requires us to replace them with new ones, which starts the process all over again: taking resources, making products out of them and sending them to landfill when we are done with them.

LEARNING FROM NATURE

A lot of things in the universe are naturally circular: the planets, Earth's rotation around the sun, Nature's processes such as the water cycle. Nature is just one big circle. And so perhaps it's time to take a leaf out of Nature's book (which did pretty well on its own for 4.6 billion years) and turn away from a linear economy to a circular one. Thankfully, many parts of the world are already doing exactly that.

CIRCLE OF LIFE

Before the Industrial Revolution in the 18th century, humans lived as part of Nature's circular system. And we can again. Our next industrial revolution is going to be one of sustainability – reducing pollution and waste at the same time as restoring Nature's balance. A revolution in which we give back as much as we take from Earth, and we help repair the damage we've done. A revolution driven by a circular economy.

SQUAWK!
The easiest materials to recycle are paper and cardboard, glass, plastics and metals.

THE TRANSITION

Reuse, repair and recycling are key parts of the transition from a linear economy to a circular one. They keep current products and materials within the loop of manufacturing for as long as possible, but there is still waste in the end. The delaying of a product being wasted is a good thing, but to become truly circular requires much more.

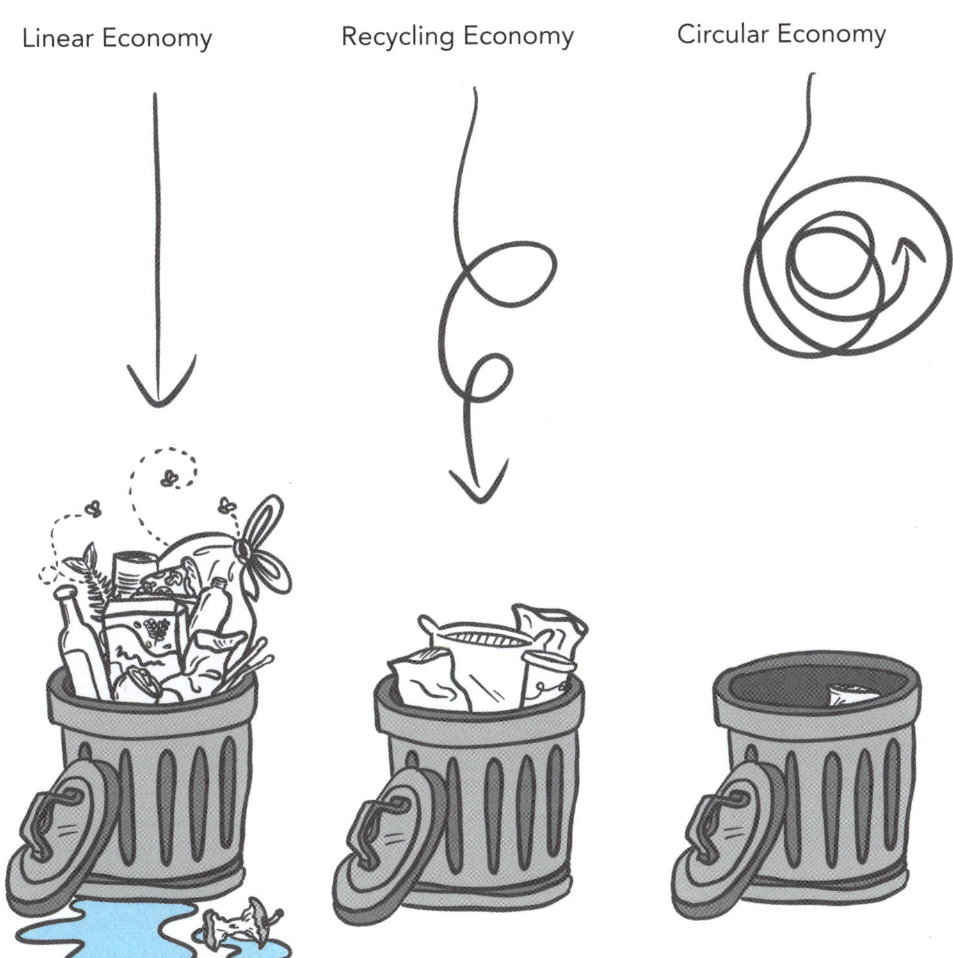

TRADITIONAL KNOWLEDGE

The circular economy is nothing new to Indigenous communities around the world. The traditions of Aboriginal and Torres Strait Islander peoples have always worked in balance with Nature, and so it is important to learn from the traditional knowledge of Australia's ancient lands to help the human systems become circular – by keeping Nature's balance at the heart of everything we do.

CIRCULAR ECONOMY

The system that dictates how goods and services are produced, sold, and bought in a country or region is called the economy, and it's that system that has a big impact on how the human world works. To achieve a circular economy, humans need to remove waste. Which means there needs to be a massive change in how we think about new products, as well as how we make them and use them.

DESIGN AND MAKE

USE

REUSE AND REPAIR

RECYCLE

1. Products and their packaging need to be made from eco-friendly materials that won't pollute Earth, and designed to be long-lasting and recyclable. Making all packaging reusable or recyclable is a great way to start the transition to a circular economy.

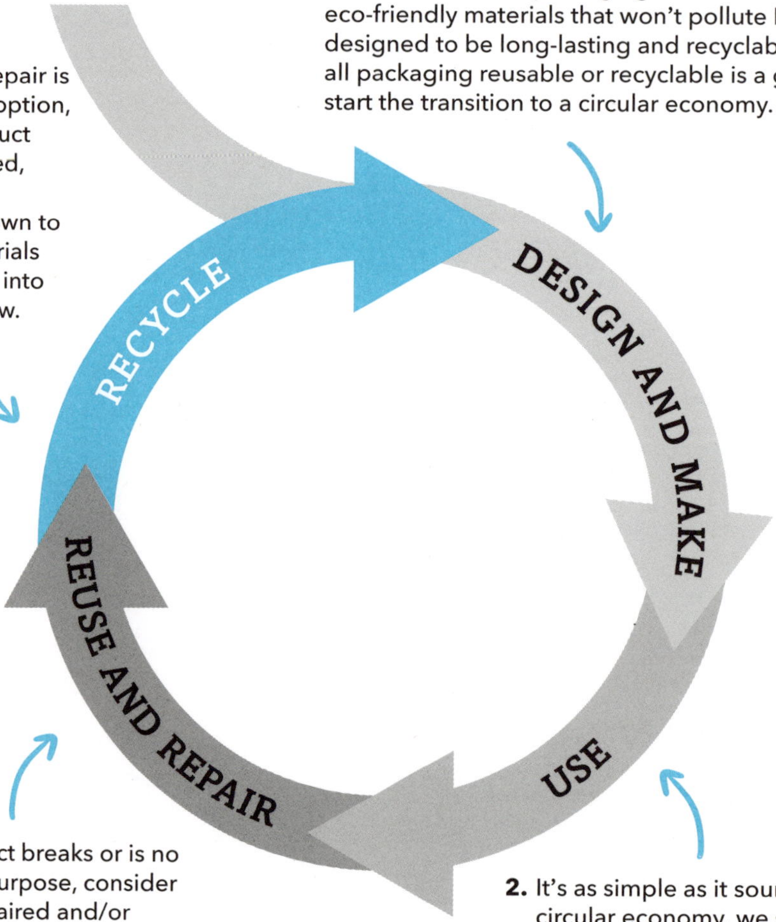

2. It's as simple as it sounds: in a circular economy, we should aim to use products for as long as possible. That means we need to stop throwing stuff away if it can still be used!

3. When a product breaks or is no longer fit for purpose, consider if it can be repaired and/or reused. This could be as simple as passing on clothes you've outgrown to a younger sibling or patching up a hole.

4. If reuse and repair is no longer an option, then the product can be recycled, which means breaking it down to its basic materials and making it into something new.

DID YOU KNOW?

Bamboo is a great eco-friendly material. It is highly sustainable as it can grow up to 90 centimetres a day, making it the fastest growing plant in the world. It is naturally strong yet light, making it versatile and useful for many human products. Because it's a plant it absorbs carbon dioxide, and it produces 35% more oxygen than other trees – making it a really good alternative material to use. Many products can be made out of bamboo, such as plates and bowls, toothbrushes and even bed sheets.

> "Waste isn't waste until it's wasted."
>
> Planet Ark

THE GOOD NEWS
SEEING THE LIGHT

The sun is the source of all energy on Earth, and so converting sunlight into electricity to power our lives is a no-brainer. Thanks to the amount of sunshine Australia enjoys, solar energy (energy from the sun) is one of Australia's leading forms of renewable energy, with solar panels installed on many houses and commercial buildings across Australia. But what happens when those solar panels break or need replacing?

SEEING DOUBLE

Logan City Council in Queensland used land available around their Loganholme Wastewater Treatment Plant to double the amount of solar energy it was producing. This not only allowed them to power their own operations, but also another incredible renewable energy innovation (turn over the page to see that amazing story).

THE BREAKDOWN

Solar panels last about 20 years before they need to be replaced, and it is estimated that Australia will generate 145,000 tonnes of solar waste by 2030. Thankfully, to prevent those solar panels from being wasted in landfill, recycling facilities are able to recycle 100% of the materials. The good thing about solar panels is that they are easily recyclable as they can be broken down into different parts without the help of chemicals, making it a clean and easy process to reduce their waste impact.

THE SUM OF THEIR PARTS

Solar panels are just as valuable when they're broken as when they're working on your roof. This is because they are made from incredibly valuable materials – including silver, aluminium, copper and silicon – that can be reused over and over again in many different ways without degrading.

SQUAWK!
Aluminium is a material that never deteriorates in quality, which means it can be recycled again and again for infinity!

1

Outer casings are removed:
Including the frame, cables and other pieces of plastic and metal.

2

Panel is processed:
Different methods are used to break down all the different raw materials.

3

Raw materials are separated:
Each group of raw materials needs to be clean of any other in order to be reusable.

4

Ready for reuse:
The different raw materials might be turned into cans, wires or new solar panels.

THE GOOD NEWS
POO POWER

Did you know there is power in poo? Energy and nutrients that the human body can't use are literally flushed down the toilet. But what if that energy could be harnessed? Scientists have found a way to do just that, to convert our number twos into electricity. Power plants that use animal manure to create electricity have existed for decades in the UK, USA and Netherlands, and now that technology is being used in Australia, to do the same with human waste.

TWO BIRDS, ONE STONE

The city of Logan in Queensland had a costly problem: more than 40 trucks a week thundered through town carrying sewage sludge to a power plant 40 kilometres away for treatment. They were costly to the environment with the amount of diesel used to fuel the trucks, they were costly to the community due to the amount of noise and pollution produced by those trucks, and they were costly to the council in dollars spent. And so, instead of trucking the waste out of town, a biosolids gasification plant was built locally to first dry out the poo before burning it in a furnace that captures the gas released and partly powers the facility. What's left after the burning is a substance called biochar, which can be used in farming as a fertiliser or in construction as building material.

SQUAWK! Logan is the first place in the Southern Hemisphere to turn human waste into energy.

Biochar is the substance left behind following burning.

Biochar is collected and used as fertiliser or in building.

FART-MOBILE

It is predicted that livestock are behind 14% of the world's greenhouse gas emissions. But what if that gas could be caught and used? UK company Bennamann has led the way in producing equipment that can be used on farms to capture the greenhouse gas methane from poo pits (or slurry pits, as farmers call them) and turn it into a clean, usable type of energy to fuel a farm's tractors. And US company New Holland is taking it one step further by developing a methane-powered generator to produce electricity that covers all of a farm's energy needs.

SQUAWK!
Poo is a highly renewable resource; where there are humans or cows, there is poo!

THE GOOD NEWS
CHANGING MINDS

With circular economy being key to our planet's future, it makes sense to be teaching the next generation of humans about how it works, and how we make it part of our lives. Hillbrook Anglican School in Queensland is leading the way by aiming to integrate circular economy education into the curriculum for its students.

LEADING THE WAY

Inspired by a talk by Planet Ark's Chief Sustainability Adviser on circular economy, science teacher Ginnese Johnston took matters into her own hands, and designed and implemented a curriculum that embeds circular economy into the school through both teaching it and doing it. Hillbrook's goal is to be 90% circular in all of its operations and practices by 2030, and they are already well on their way to achieving this through performing waste audits and installing a digital water meter and solar panels (with the help of Plant Ark Power).

> **Problem solving and thinking outside the box are necessary skills for solving many sustainability issues.**
>
> Ginnese Johnston, science teacher, Hillbrook Anglican School

REAL-LIFE SKILLS

The lessons that are taught at the school empower students to find sustainable solutions to waste problems in their immediate environment. One project's aim for some Year 10 students was to process the food scraps from the school's tuckshop, and the students put together a test version of an anaerobic digester, which transforms food waste into usable biogas and soil fertiliser.

WIDENING THE SCOPE

The main goal of including circular economy education in schools is to ensure it's a part of the way students approach problem solving. Science has always required skills such as investigation, discussion and asking questions, with the main goal of science to find answers to some of life's biggest questions, one of which is our planet's sustainable future. Schools across Australia can become a part of the Sustainable Schools Network to share knowledge and resources to make our future a sustainable one.

THE GOOD NEWS
EDUCATING BY DESIGN

As more businesses move towards a more circular way of working, it's essential they are able to get informed advice on the design and development of new processes, products and – most importantly – packaging. Thankfully, in Australia and New Zealand, that's where PREP comes in . . .

DOING YOUR PREP

The Packaging Recyclability Evaluation Portal – or PREP for short – has been revolutionary in helping designers make the packaging of their products fully recyclable, based on the recycling measures available in Australia and New Zealand. Coded with the knowledge about what can be recycled in ANZ and how, the computer program checks the materials used in the packaging and spits out a report that designers can then use to fix the bits that need fixing to make something fully recyclable.

HOW DOES IT WORK?

There are lots of different parts to packaging, and every element is important in considering its recyclability. And so designers need to check everything, from the ink and glue used to the shape, size and weight. PREP makes this checking process a lot easier for designers, and the best part is that they can do it from the start of the process, before anything is created, preventing waste from the very beginning.

HOW ARE MATERIALS RECYCLED?

The method used to recycle is different for each product. Aluminium cans are shredded then melted before being moulded into something new. Paper, on the other hand, is put in a watery bath of chemicals that break it down into a slurry, which is then filtered and cleaned and made into reams of new paper. These processes are fairly simple compared to what's needed to recycle some plastics. And some processes are so complicated that we don't yet have the technology to separate out the different materials, so for now those products are non-recyclable. This is why incorporating sustainability into the design of products is so important, as well as investing in research to create the technology that will one day allow everything to be recycled.

THE GOOD NEWS
IT'S ALL IN THE LABEL

Designing recyclable products and packaging is the first step, but how can we be sure they get recycled properly, especially when different councils around Australia have different rules about what can be recycled through kerbside collections? The solution is the Australasian Recycling Label (ARL).

AUSTRALASIAN RECYCLING LABEL

The ARL was launched in 2018 and is a proven system that is directly linked to the PREP process to make it easier to know how to recycle different elements of packaging. With the help of Planet Ark, easily understandable labels are now printed on more than 255,000 products that Australians buy.

A piece of packaging could consist of many parts, such as a lid, foil wrapper and the box or container itself. Each component could be one of these three types – recyclable, conditionally recyclable or non-recyclable – and is clearly labelled as such on the ARL:

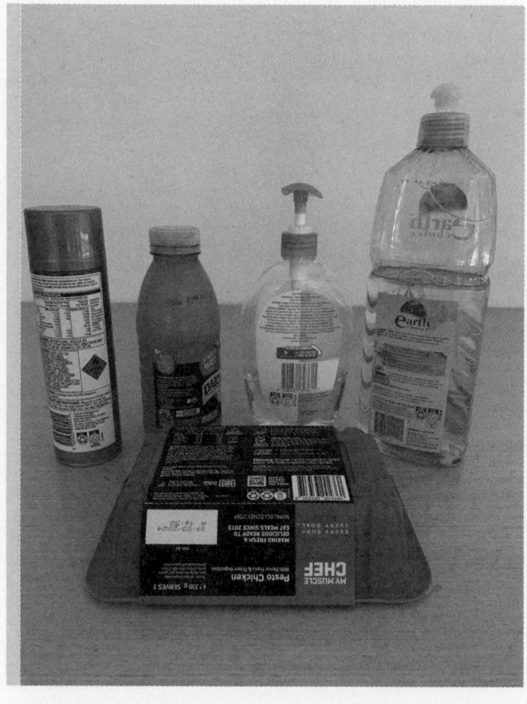

Recyclable:
Place in kerbside recycling.

Conditionally Recyclable Only:
Recycle if instructions below symbol are followed.

Package Component:
Shows specific part of packaging that can't be recycled.

BEYOND THE LABEL

The ARL has helped companies around Australia and New Zealand design for recyclability from the very beginning of the design phase – and if something isn't recyclable, it is made clear on the label. By using the ARL, the aim is to have properly sorted and separated materials being sent for recycling so they can be used again without going to landfill.

ACCOUNTABILITY

The Australian government has committed to making businesses accountable in doing their part to make Australia's packaging circular in its usage with National Packaging Targets to be met by 2025:

- Packaging to be 100% reusable, recyclable or compostable.
- 70% of plastic packaging to be recycled or composted.
- 50% of recycled content to be made into packaging materials.
- Phase out plastic packaging that is difficult to recycle, and unnecessary single-use plastics packaging.

THE GOOD NEWS
INK OUTSIDE THE BOX

Recyclable items can be broken down and their different materials separated, which can then be used to create something new. So a product's recyclability doesn't only depend on the materials it's made from, but also on whether the technology exists to break it down and separate the materials for recycling.

YOU CAN RECYCLE MORE THAN YOU THINK

Just because there isn't a collection point for something doesn't mean it can't be recycled at all. Recycling is all about finding a new purpose for old and existing materials, so they don't go to waste. Luckily, most of the items we use today can be recycled in one form or another. It's all about putting that little extra effort into finding out how.

MAKING A MARK

One item that is recyclable, but you might not realise, is a printer cartridge. Many of the materials in a printer cartridge are toxic to ground soil when in landfill, and so recycling those materials – which include plastics, metal, ink and toner – is a game changer for the planet.

Cartridges 4 Planet Ark is a recycling program set up in 2003 that has provided a free and convenient recycling solution for printer cartridges and accessories across Australia. Schools, workplaces, community centres and retail stores can all sign up to be collection points to recycle cartridges.

NEW FOR OLD

While recycling some items means they are made into new versions of the same thing, other materials are capable of being used for new purposes. In partnership with sustainable solution provider Close the Loop, the Cartridges 4 Planet Ark program has collected old cartridges and helped break down the different materials ready for them to be used to make multiple new products. Some became new cartridges, others became fences or new road surfaces.

NOT SO LOUSY INK

Lousy Ink is a community art collective that started up in Melbourne in 2017, supporting local artists by offering exhibition space and bringing a sustainable solution to the waste ink that can't be recycled by printer cartridge manufacturers themselves. Lousy Ink puts the waste ink to use in pens, illustration ink and other art supplies, which are all packaged in recyclable materials. Lousy Ink have repurposed more than 85,000 litres of ink in this way. Keeping ink in circulation eliminates the risk of it damaging the environment, allowing us to make the most of useful resources.

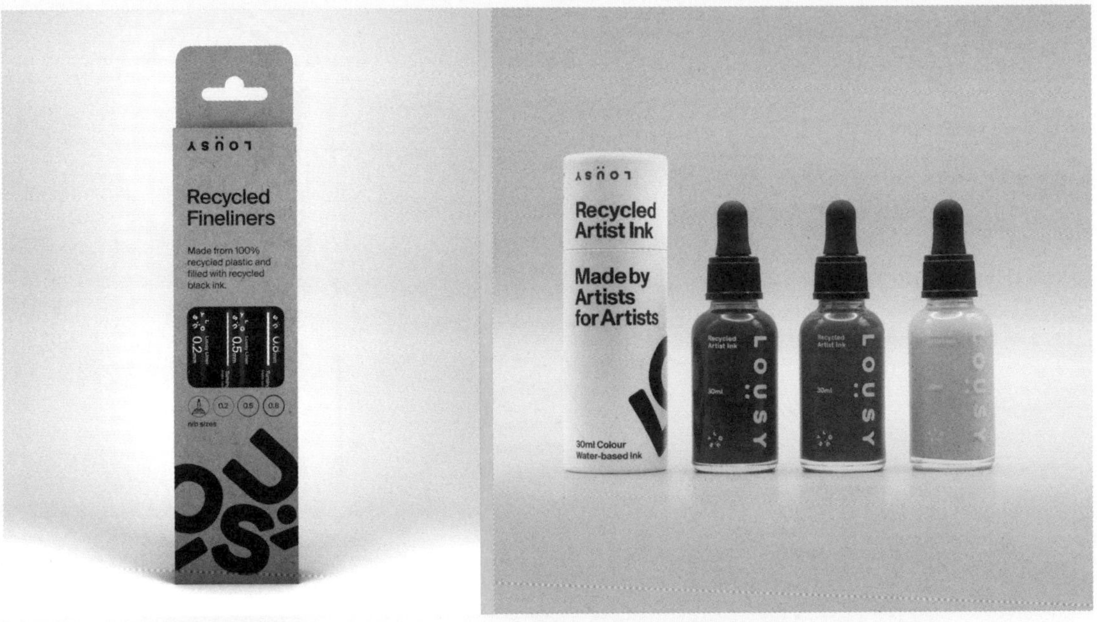

THE GOOD NEWS

OLD SCHOOL STUFF

More than two-thirds of textiles in Australia end up in landfill, and it is estimated that every school in Australia throws away between 100kg and 200kg of uniforms each year! In response to these confronting statistics, organisations around the country are turning that waste back into useful resources. How resourceful is that?

OLD UNIFORMS, NEW LIFE

Australia has more than 9000 schools that send an estimated 2000 tonnes of uniforms to landfill every year. In 2020, Annie Thompson, founder of Sustainable Schoolwear and Worn Up, started collecting and transforming uniform fibres into a new material to stop them going to landfill. More than 100 schools, 13 councils and corporations signed up to the nation-wide test program, with 84 tonnes of uniforms collected in a year for transformation into a new material.

HOW IT WORKS

Starting out with a pizza oven and car press in her backyard, Annie and her partner Murray began experimenting. Two years, three pizza ovens and a move into a warehouse later, they had transformed the materials into Australia's first waste-based composite material – FABTEC. The material was tested and given top marks by CSIRO, Australia's national science agency. Then, the FABTEC prototypes were used to make desktops and stool-tops, all out of recycled uniforms! These were snapped up by Worn Up's pioneer customers, such as IKEA Australia and Lowes, as well as the schools that had participated in the initial testing. FABTEC is now turned into desks, tables, partitions and furniture, and can be upcycled five times without losing any quality. Annie calls these 'desks for life' because customers can send them back for upcycling again into a new desk.

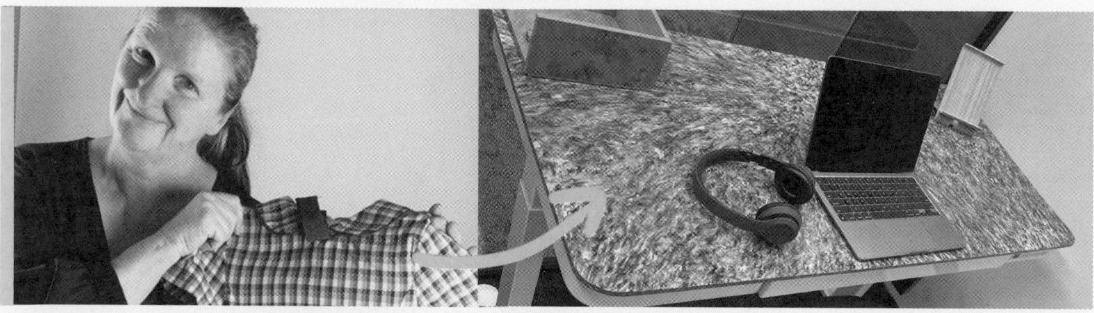

QUALITY BEATS QUANTITY

Worn Up's sister organisation, Sustainable Schoolwear, helps schools and students reduce their environmental impact by giving them access to uniforms that are made ethically, locally (wherever possible) and from high-quality sustainable materials. The quality is the key to becoming more circular, because quality clothes last longer and also create better-quality products when they are finally recycled.

MORE GOOD NEWS

Worn Up has also partnered with Macquarie University's Deep Tech Lab and The City of Ryde Council to create The Worn Up Textile Innovation Lab, which is aiming to create more materials from the textile resources we once called waste and share information to help others do the same.

MAKING UNIFORMS FROM PLASTIC BOTTLES

While Worn Up has been giving old uniforms new life on Australia's east coast, a small sports store from Joondalup, a northern suburb of Perth, has been making new uniforms out of old plastic bottles on the west coast. The recycled fabric is being used to create school uniforms and sports kits of the same quality as regular sports gear – with the bonus that it's a whole lot better for the environment. Using recycled polyester sourced from recycled plastic bottles keeps that plastic out of landfill and prevents the use of more natural resources. According to Mecca Sports, using recycled polyester to make clothing also uses 20% less energy and 85% less water than creating new polyester from fossil fuels, and the carbon dioxide emissions from the recycled version are drastically lower, too. That is very good news!

THE GOOD NEWS

FANTASTIC PLASTIC?

First created in 1907, plastic is one of the human race's most useful inventions – it is strong yet lightweight and highly durable. It has also proved cheap and easy to make, so plastic has replaced other more expensive natural materials, like wood and metal, in products all around the world. But plastic has also become a tough problem for our Earth . . .

HOW PLASTIC IS MADE

Plastic is a human-made product, made using chemicals that come from fossil fuels such as oil and gas. It can be moulded into any shape and is in just about everything that we use, from lunchboxes and drink bottles to swimming goggles and thongs. It can even be made into fine strands that can be woven into fabrics (such as polyester) and used to make clothes. There are more than 50 different types of plastic.

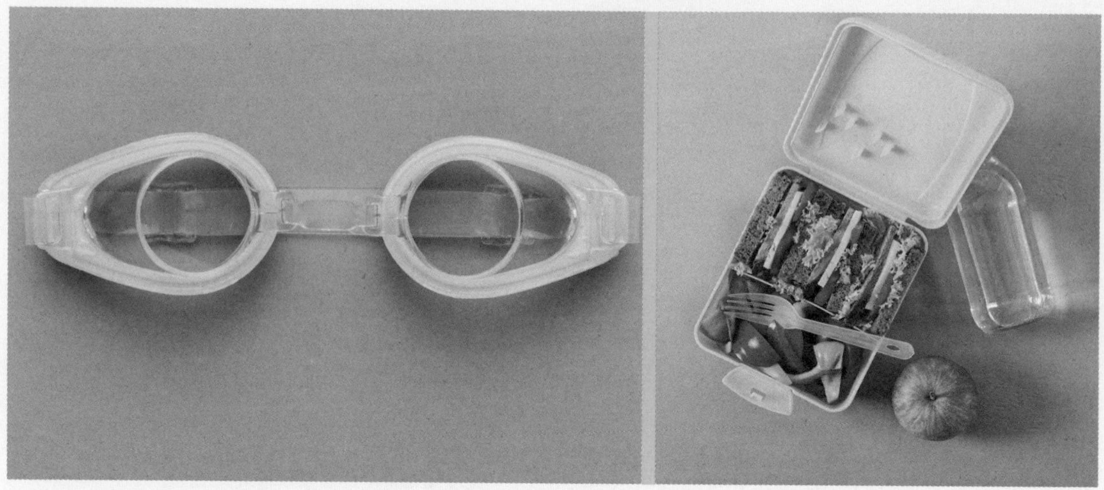

WHAT'S THE PROBLEM?

Plastic is usually made from fossil fuels which, as we explained in Chapter 2, take millions of years to be made and are a limited resource – they will run out. Using such precious resources in products like food wrappers that are used once and then thrown away is extremely wasteful. And plastic, being so tough, does not break down easily. Instead of decomposing, it simply breaks up into tiny pieces called microplastics, which escape into Nature and poison food chains. It can take centuries for plastic to fully decompose.

WHAT'S THE SOLUTION?

Thankfully, the plastic used in bottles, which is one of the most common plastic products, can be recycled through council kerbside pick-ups or through container deposit schemes, making it very easy for us to recycle. But not all plastic is the same, and so it needs to be recycled in different ways, which is why you can't put all plastic in your recycling bin.You may have noticed numbers from 1 to 7 in a triangle on products. These classify the different types of plastics. Most councils accept numbers 1, 2 and 5.

HOW IS PLASTIC RECYCLED?

That plastic bottle you threw in the recycling bin has a long journey ahead. From the recycling truck to the recycling plant, the bottle will be tossed, sorted, cleaned, shredded and maybe even melted. The tiny bits of plastic that were once a bottle can then be used to make all sorts of things, like T-shirts and sneakers, carpets and cups.

BIOPLASTICS

Some companies have started making materials out of plants, such as corn or sugar cane, rather than fossil fuels, in an attempt to make them a more sustainable part of the planet's future. While making bioplastic is a more costly operation and the recycling of bioplastic requires a separate process from the fossil fuel-based plastics, using plants means the plastic contains less chemicals and toxins and they can be composted in specialised facilities at high heat. Australia is starting to invest in more of these facilities, but reusables will always be a better option than common bioplastic products like cups, plates and bowls used for takeaway food and drink.

MORE GOOD NEWS

In 2021, the Australian government committed to a National Plastics Plan to reduce plastic waste, increase recycling rates and find alternatives to plastic.

THE GOOD NEWS
PLASTIC TRANSFORMED

With a little creativity, items destined for the bin can be transformed into something new and given a second life. This is particularly important for plastic products, as plastic breaks down into a weaker version of itself every time it is processed into something new. Finding new ways to use it in its original form is better for everyone – plastic included.

FROM POLLUTION TO ART

Sydney-based conceptual artist Marina DeBris loves the beach, but hates the trash that washes up there. On her daily runs, she started picking up items to help clean up, but more just kept appearing day after day. Marina started to use the trash to create pieces of art. In doing so, Marina has not only given the rubbish a new life, she's also helping to educate people about pollution through her artworks, and challenging them to reflect on their own wasteful behaviours. Her 'trashion' outfits are created from items washed up on beaches, and her installation The Inconvenience Store cleverly displays products that ended up in the ocean as junk, showing how inconvenient plastic waste is to ocean life.

DID YOU KNOW?

Most pool toys are made from a tough type of plastic called polyvinyl chloride, or PVC for short. This sturdy, flexible and weather-resistant material takes an estimated 1000 years to break down, and when it does break down it becomes microplastics that get into the food chain and poison wildlife. PVC also contains toxic chemicals, which are harmful to human health as well as the environment.

POOL TOYS

They're brightly coloured and fun to splash around the pool with, but inflatable pool toys are no fun once the air is taken out of them. Or are they? Queensland couple Carin van Gunsven and Gerhard Sandker accumulated a bunch of old pool toys in their backyard from their three splashy kids, but the fact that the broken toys were heading to landfill upset the climate-conscious pair. Using their creative skills, they fashioned the old inflatables into new usable items, including bags and pencil cases, and the small business Ploys Designs was born. The company now takes donated pool inflatables and repurposes them into fun new items for people to buy Australia-wide. Word of their colourful eye-catching designs soon gained them customers and their range has expanded to include earrings, and laptop and phone cases. More than 250 kilograms of donated pool inflatables have been saved from landfill. They've even upcycled a children's jumping castle!

POOL TOYS OF THE FUTURE

More than 2.5 million people in Australia live in a house with a swimming pool. That's a lot of people, a lot of pools and a lot of pool inflatables. Thankfully, there is an alternative to those made out of PVC. More are being made using natural materials, such as bamboo fibre and cornstarch.

MORE GOOD NEWS

Some governments around the world have already banned PVC and its products in their countries.

THE GOOD NEWS

DESIGNED BY NATURE

Nature is the very best designer and the very best problem-solver, and so it makes sense to look to Nature when designing new things. From the built environment to the colours on our cars, nature-inspired design – also known as biomimicry – is becoming more and more popular with designers of products and the people who use them. And the fact that research has found Nature is a crucial part of people living happy and healthy lives is the cherry on the cake.

SQUAWK!
Biophilia is the word used to describe the fact that people are naturally inclined to connect with Nature.

HOOKED

The well-known and loved hook-and-loop fastener, Velcro®, was inspired by the seeds of the Burdock plant, which hook on to animal fur to be spread and grow away from the parent plant. While walking in the Alps in the 1940s, Swiss engineer George de Mestral found these seeds hooked in his woolly clothes, which planted the seed of an idea – a fastening system based on the hooks of the Burdock seeds and the tiny loops of animal fur.

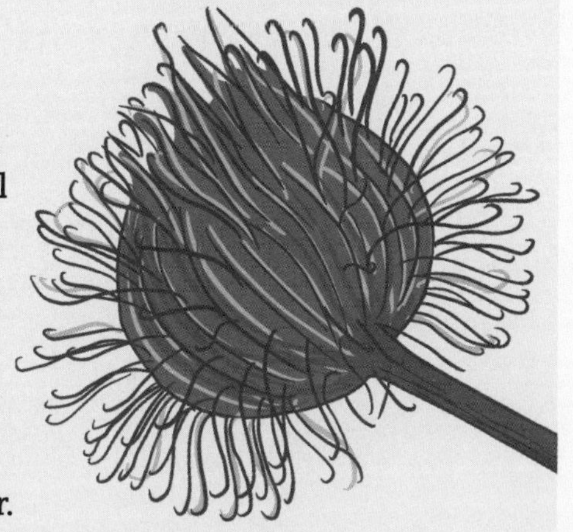

BUILDING DESIGN

Wood is one of the oldest building materials, as well as one of the most naturally beautiful. Responsibly sourced timber materials are a natural and renewable resource, which makes the building industry more sustainable and helps combat climate change:

- As trees grow, they absorb carbon dioxide from the atmosphere, and approximately 50% of the weight of wood is carbon, which remains locked in the wood for the life of the product.
- Using more wood in buildings instead of materials such as aluminium, steel and concrete significantly reduces the carbon emissions in the construction industry.

RESPONSIBLY SOURCED WOOD

When using timber to build, it is imperative that the wood is responsibly sourced from a certified forest. This means the wood is specifically grown and harvested for building materials in specially managed forests that are replanted to ensure a constant stream of materials that does not interfere with natural parks and forests. In doing so, the environmental benefits of plants and trees such as producing oxygen, filtering the air, and removing carbon from the atmosphere are not interrupted.

MELBOURNE SCHOOL OF DESIGN

Opened in 2014, the Melbourne School of Design adopted nature-inspired design into the building of its learning space to reflect the local climate. The designers achieved this by utilising natural ventilation, daylight and optimal sun shading to create an environment inside that reacts to and reflects the natural environment outside. The mostly timber space provides people with some of the benefits that come with working in a natural environment, such as stress reduction, improved concentration, improved mood and an overall more positive attitude.

PAINTLESS PAINT

Did you know that the stunningly vivid colours of many butterflies' wings are actually produced by the interplay between two colourless materials that make up the scales? An innovative team at the US University of Central Florida drew inspiration from this fact to create the world's first environmentally friendly paintless 'paint'. The key to creating colour is in how the two materials are structured together in specific patterns to reflect and absorb light in a particular way that emits just one colour in the light spectrum. The paint is a lightweight alternative to pigment-based paints, and has already been used on some cars.

ECO TIP

Look around you while you walk to school and ride your bike to the park. Are there are any parts of nature that could inspire an improvement to something you use in your life? Sometimes, it's the simplest ideas that work the best and are the most sustainable.

Social Innovation

SOCIAL INNOVATION

Social inclusion is a part of the circular economy that is often overlooked. The human world is generally seen as separate to Nature at best, and working against it at worst, but the key to a successfully circular future is to ensure the human and natural worlds work together cohesively – not separate or in parallel. A sustainable future therefore MUST address human social needs as well as environmental needs. And this chapter celebrates the people who are already doing innovative things to achieve just that.

MONEY MAKES THE WORLD GO ROUND

The planet is clearly facing an environmental crisis. So why are countries and the businesses within them often slow to react and change? Rightly or wrongly, there is a perception that it costs more to be environmentally friendly. Products marked as eco-friendly are perceived to be more expensive than similar items, even when in reality they are simply accounting for costs to the environment that have always been there. It is the same case with Earth's natural resources. Coal and oil supplies were once thought plentiful and were therefore cheap. There is also the fact that the technologies we developed rely on using fossil fuels, so these are often cheaper and easier to use than alternatives. Of course, the cost of this is the health of the environment.

HEALTHY ECONOMY

Making money is a factor holding back many countries from going green. Earth's natural resources are extremely valuable now that they're in short supply, and certain countries (including Australia) have lots of them. Australia is the world's largest exporter of coal, which means other countries pay Australia money for its coal. Making the choice to stop mining coal due to the damage it does to the environment might therefore impact the health of the country's economy in the short term, even if it's for the best in the long term for both the economy and the environment.

THE COST OF DOING GOOD

The materials needed to make environmentally friendly products, as well as the manufacturing processes to create them, can be more expensive than conventional approaches. The reason petroleum-based plastic became the material of choice for many products during the 1900s was because petroleum (oil) was low-cost, and plastic was quick and easy to make, meaning it could be sold cheaply. Eco-friendly alternatives made from renewable and recycled materials like bamboo, wood, high-quality metals and glass often take more time to grow or extract and can therefore cost more to produce. However, fossil fuels are becoming harder and more expensive to extract as we use up existing supplies, and waiting to transition until these are really hard to find will be more expensive than doing it now.

WHERE IN THE WORLD?

Different countries around the world have different levels of wealth. Australia is extremely privileged to be one of the planet's richest countries. It makes sense, then, for Australia to be investing in green economies as part of the global community, because it can afford to. Even with the stark disparity between the poorest and richest communities in Australia, there is still a choice of eco-friendly products that those who can afford it can choose. In contrast, in many of the poorest nations, such as on the African continent, people struggle with basic human needs, including housing, clean drinking water and food. They have to make do with the products they can afford, whether they're eco-friendly or not. Choice is a privilege they do not have. And this is why it is important for rich nations to do more than their fair share of green investments – to help make up for those who can't.

Australia is the world's third richest nation per adult. Democratic Republic of Congo is the world's poorest nation per adult.

Average Australian wage:
$83,200 a year
which is **$228** a day

Average DRC wage:
$394.25 a year
which is **$1.80** a day

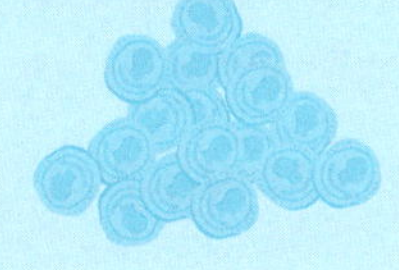

ECO TIP

Even though some eco-friendly products are expensive to buy, they can often save you money in the long run. Many eco-friendly items can be reused again and again due to their better quality materials, meaning you don't have to replace eco-friendly items as often as plastic versions.

THE GOOD NEWS
WEALTH FROM WASTE

Did you know that most of the materials we throw in the bin are still valuable resources? Almost everything can be reused or recycled to create something new, and yet, on average, every Australian throws away 2.7 tonnes of materials per year. That's a lot of valuable resources sitting in a hole in the ground. To help educate and motivate people, many government-led programs and schemes are offering rewards to help people make the conscious choice to waste less, recycle more.

THE BIGGEST INFLUENCER

Money has been proven time and again to be an influential factor in getting people to do things they wouldn't usually do – such as taking empty drink containers to a recycling centre instead of dropping them in the nearest bin. The hope with money-for-waste schemes is that the eco-friendly actions become a person's natural good habits that continue even when the person isn't receiving a reward.

Container Deposit Schemes (CDS) are one type of recycling program where you can return your used bottles, cans or cartons to certain stores in exchange for cash. With each container returned you can earn 10 cents, which is a great way to get some pocket money while also reducing litter in the environment. The containers returned through CDS can then be turned into new products like cans, bottles and packaging.

CARBON CURRENCY

A carbon credit is a type of permit or allowance where each credit represents one tonne of carbon dioxide. Carbon credits can be created through any project that reduces carbon, like tree planting, and can be sold to another company to balance out their greenhouse gas emissions. A company that emits one tonne of carbon dioxide can offset that by buying one carbon credit from another company that has the credit.

This can also be a way to encourage companies to reduce their emissions. For example, rather than using carbon credits to offset their emissions, a company can decide to not pollute the environment in the first place and then sell their stored carbon credits to someone else for a profit. The carbon credit scheme aims to share the load between businesses so that the carbon that companies emit into the atmosphere is balanced out by the carbon that other companies remove.

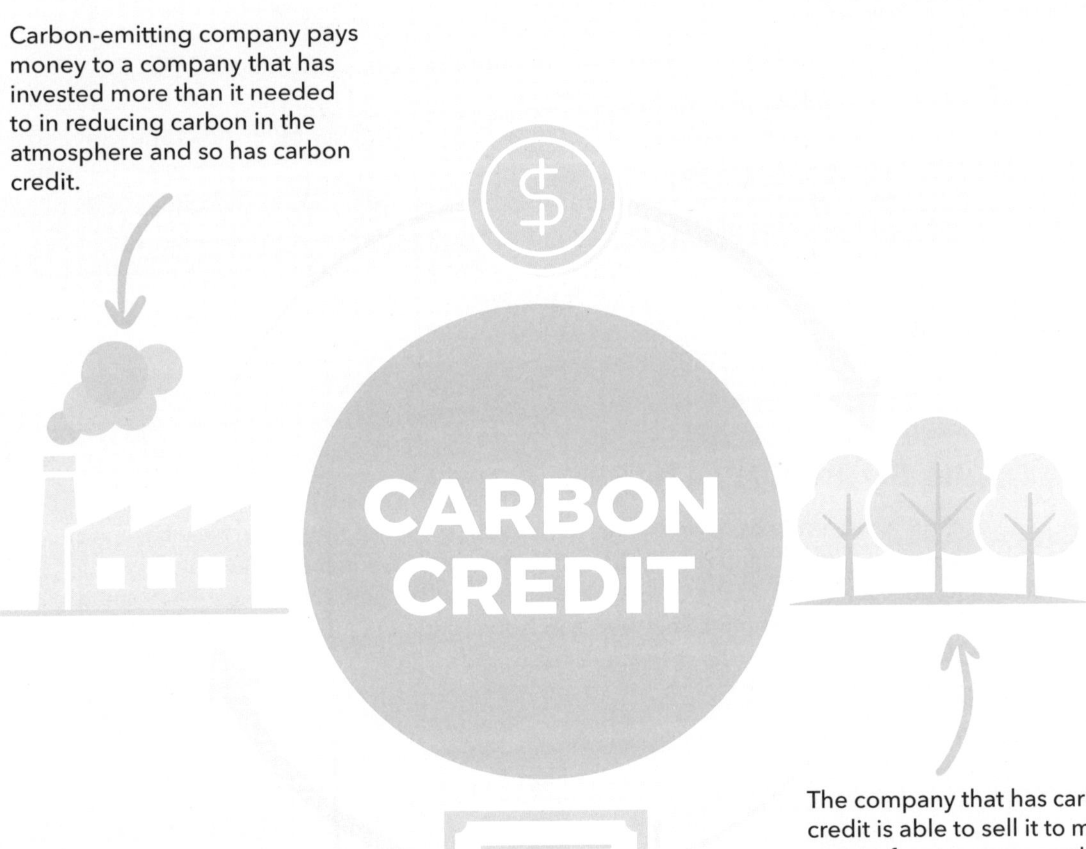

THE GOOD NEWS

LITTLE SCHOOL, BIG DEEDS

In many remote Australian communities, kerbside recycling doesn't exist. Remote towns are often a long way away from recycling plants and have small populations, and so councils often deem the cost too high to provide a recycling service. Unhappy with the lack of recycling opportunities in their community, a group of primary school students from Manyallaluk in the Northern Territory took matters into their own hands to save resources from landfill, raise money for the community and protect their beautiful home.

MAKING MONEY

The small school in Manyallaluk has around 25 students from preschool to Year Six. These students all take part in the school's curriculum that is focused on the environmental benefits of recycling as well as the social benefits it creates in keeping the community clean, working as a team and, thanks to the Cash for Containers scheme, making money. To begin, the students first worked together to source collection bins, which were installed on the school grounds. Once the bins are full, the students make a list of what they have and calculate the amount of money they'll receive once the containers are taken the 100 kilometres to the Container Deposit Scheme (CDS) in Katherine.

CASH FOR CONTAINERS

In 2012, the Northern Territory introduced a container deposit scheme to keep beverage containers out of landfill and reduce litter. Called Cash for Containers, the scheme was first introduced in South Australia and is now operating in every one of Australia's states. A 10-cent deposit is added to all beverages in stores, and then juice boxes, drink bottles and cans are all eligible for that 10-cent deposit-return when the customer brings back the container for recycling.

SQUAWK!
Australia is the first continent in the world to install CDS schemes in every single state.

WILDLIFE MONITORING

Recycling initiatives are just one of the environmental projects the school is involved in. In 2020, the Manyallaluk students won a trophy for their STEM project after presenting it to scientists and environmental groups at the Northern Territory Natural Resource Management conference in Darwin. Five-year-old Manyallaluk student Jai Maralngurra was the youngest presenter to speak about their project, which involved monitoring the nearby creek for buffalo throughout the year using the school's drone. The school is now involved in monitoring a whole host of wildlife, using spy cameras to search for Gouldian finches and using a GoPro camera to see what lives in the creek.

BRINGING THE SHADE

The students also participated in National Tree Day, planting trees with funding from Planet Ark's Seedling Bank. The shade of these trees will allow for communities to gather and connect out of the heat of the harsh sun, while also providing habitat and shelter for the range of wildlife that inhabits Central Arnhem Land. These meeting places are important for the community. Everyone is both a teacher and a student at Manyallaluk.

> "The kids and families teach us their language, stories and skills, and they show us their Country. The richness of this culture and traditional knowledge is something that we consider an immense privilege to learn from."

Principal Kleinig,
Manyallaluk Primary School

THE GOOD NEWS
HAIRY PROBLEMS

Australian hair salons send more than 400,000 kilograms of hair to landfill each year, and one million kilograms of foil. Foil can be easily recycled, while hair can take a long time to decompose – usually years. And, if it's left in plastic bags while it breaks down, hair can produce the damaging greenhouse gas, methane. Thankfully, hairdresser Paul Frasca and environmentalist Ewelina Soroko teamed up and found eco-friendly solutions to deal with all that unwanted hair and salon waste.

DID YOU KNOW?
Profit-for-Purpose organisations are businesses with a social purpose. They reinvest any profits made back into achieving that social purpose.

LEARNING FROM THEIR CLIENTS

On a four-month car journey around Australia and after visiting 160 salons, Paul and Ewelina came up with an idea to create an online salon directory and waste removal service in order to make the hairdressing industry more sustainable. First of all, they focused on recycling the foil and set up the industry's first recycled foil product, Refoil, in 2010. Then, in 2015, they launched Profit-for-Purpose organisation, Sustainable Salons, which recycles 95% of salon waste for their users in Australia.

Aluminium foil is used a lot in salons during hair colouring. Sustainable Salons collects the foil and processes it into newly cut pieces ready to be sold back to salons.

Plastic, such as from shampoo and conditioner bottles, is collected and repurposed into combs, climbing hooks, coasters, plant pots and even frames for glasses.

Long hair is sent to wig makers to assist cancer and alopecia sufferers who have lost their own hair.

Short hair, collected into bundles called 'hair booms', can be used to mop up oil spills.

Paper and cardboard from all the magazines and hair-product packaging is also collected.

Chemicals, including peroxide used in colouring hair, are processed to either rebalance the liquid into usable recycled water or are disposed of by incineration. Nothing is sent to landfill and nothing goes down the drain into our waterways.

SQUAWK!

1 kilogram of hair can remove 840 grams of spilled oil from seawater.

ECO TIP

There are lots of chemicals in soaps, shampoo and cleaning products used in bathrooms. Look for natural options that are less polluting to waterways.

MORE GOOD NEWS

Human hair contains lots of essential nutrients, including nitrogen, calcium and iron. It is therefore a brilliant ingredient to add to your compost heap, and is already being added to enrich some soil fertilisers.

THE GOOD NEWS

SUSTAINABLE EATING

Eating food together is one of our favourite things. Sharing a meal is extremely sociable and often centres around celebrations. But how we get our food in the current system is no cause for celebration. Thanks to our well-developed transport systems, food and its waste is transported across countries and around the world, a process that is highly damaging to the environment. Here, we look at ways some people are sourcing food in a more sustainable way.

FARM TO FORK

Also called 'farm to table', the farm to fork strategy is gaining traction on a global scale. It involves redesigning our food chain into something that works with the environment and reduces the big climate footprint of our current food system. And to ensure the human part of the circular economy is addressed, it also aims to give everyone access to nutritious, sustainable, affordable food at the same time as ensuring the farmers get a fair price.

URBAN FARMS

The idea of growing our food on unused land in cities is nothing new, and today there are long waiting lists for allotments in large city suburbs. More schools are also creating their own kitchen gardens so that kids learn the skills to grow their own food, and the benefits of it, from an early age. These farms tend to be small due to the limited space in urban areas, but productive with high-yield crops that make the most of the space. By growing our food near cafes and restaurants, a farmer and their food can be closer to customers, reducing the financial and environmental costs of transporting food to cities.

MICROFARMS

The world's largest microfarm is located on the rooftop of Paris's Exhibition Centre. The 14,000-square-metre farm produces as much as 1000 kilograms of food a day from 35 varieties of fruits and vegetables, and uses coconut fibre – which would otherwise be wasted – instead of soil. The farm supplies nearby hotels, residents and an onsite restaurant with produce. Locals can even use one of the 140 plots to grow their own plants.

THE FOOD-SCRAP CHALLENGE

In Australia, it is estimated that each person wastes almost 300 kilograms of food every year. Some chefs are stepping up to the challenge to create gourmet meals from food scraps – every bit of peel, pip, stem and off-cut is used. Didn't you know that ice cream made from potato skins with syrup from a mango stone is the new fine dining dessert? It's time to get creative in the kitchen!

Even if you do end up throwing some food away, you can throw it closer to home and ensure it isn't wasted by using it to make compost. This not only ensures that no nutrients are lost, as the compost puts those nutrients into the soil, but it also helps reduce food miles and all those greenhouse emissions that go with transport.

MORE GOOD NEWS

Some school students in Melbourne have replaced their canteen vending machine with a vertical farm that grows radish microgreens. The indoor aquaponics installation turns fish waste into nutrients for the plants, and is part of an educational program by social enterprise Farmwall that teaches the principles of circular economy, as well as the connection between climate change and food insecurity. Students plant microgreens into soggy pots and, a few weeks later, they can harvest the microgreens to take home and grow, or munch with their lunch.

THE GOOD NEWS
GOING OFF-GRID

Electricity powers just about every aspect of our modern lives. From lighting and cooling our homes and cooking our food to charging our phones and computer devices, electricity is something we very much rely on and take for granted. Imagine only having electricity for a few hours a day, or not having it at all. How would you keep food from going to waste without a fridge or freezer – let alone cook it? These are the realities of many communities in rural Australia as well as less wealthy countries around the world. Inventions that utilise off-grid energy can play an important role in reducing poverty and improving health while saving the environment.

MODERN FRIDGE, ANCIENT DESIGN

Driven by the goal of giving everyone equal access to good health, two students in Malaysia, Kuan Weiking and Theodore Garvindeo Seah, designed and developed a fridge that does not need electricity. Instead, it uses the centuries-old design of a traditional Malaysian water pitcher – a labu sayong – that keeps water cool using Earth's natural resource, clay. Clay is a naturally porous material, which means it allows air and water to pass through it, and this is key to how the Kuno (which means ancient) fridge works. The clay pot has two walls – one inner, which is baked to make it waterproof, and one outer, which is kept porous. The gap between the walls is filled with sand, an even more porous material. When the sand is wet, it cools the inner wall and anything inside it by drawing out the warm air. The outer clay wall then exacerbates the effect of the sand's cooling process by allowing warm air to escape through it so that the sand can draw more warm air from the inner wall.

DID YOU KNOW?

Refrigeration is vital for keeping food fresh, so that people get the nutrients they need to stay healthy. It is also essential for storing some medicines and vaccines.

MAKING THE MOST OF WHAT YOU HAVE

Kuno is basically a flowerpot fridge. To make the most of the water that is needed to keep the sand between the clay walls wet, soil in the top part of the pot can be used to grow plants, which are routinely watered. When watered, the plant takes what it needs from the soil, and the rest of the water flows into the sand layer of the Kuno to cool whatever is inside the 'fridge'. Kuno is made from sustainable ground material (clay and sand), and can be made by hand on a small scale, which means it can be created by those who need it as well as opening the door for them to a new sustainable way of making money.

DID YOU KNOW?
An estimated 10% of the world's population doesn't have access to electricity.

Food can be grown in the top part of the Kuno, and then fresh produce stored in the fridge compartment.

SQUAWK!
The Kuno won the 2020 James Dyson Award for design, and the H2Pro (see below) was a 2014 Google Science Fair finalist.

CLEAN WATER

Many of the 760 million people around the world who don't have access to electricity also don't have access to safe drinking water, and all of the water purifying technologies that already exist require an external source of electricity. In 2014, Australian Cynthia Sin Nga Lam invented the H2Pro to help address this. Her H2Pro design purifies wastewater and produces electricity at the same time. Powered by sunlight, the device makes the most of free, renewable energy and does not produce emissions. It works by filtering dirty water through a solar-powered titanium mesh, which sterilises the water and makes it safe for drinking. Water is made up of two hydrogen molecules and one oxygen, which is written as H_2O. The chemical reaction that removes the pollutants from the water also separates the water's hydrogen and oxygen molecules, which could then be used to power a hydrogen fuel cell to generate clean electricity.

MORE GOOD NEWS
Each state in Australia is looking at providing solar panels on social housing so that those who can't afford the costs to access electricity have a free supply.

THE GOOD NEWS
COASTAL GRAZERS

An observant farmer in Canada noticed that his dairy cows that grazed in fields on the coastline and ate the storm-tossed seaweed deposited there were healthier and produced more milk. But why? The answer is methane. And here's why it is such a big deal.

FLATULENT FARMS

The large-scale nature of farming today has a big impact on the environment. Farming is hugely affected by any changes to climate, including global warming and floods and droughts, and yet emits about a third of the world's greenhouse gases. As well as carbon dioxide, methane gas is released in agricultural processes – specifically, whenever cows, sheep and other livestock burp and fart.

GASSY PROBLEM

Although methane stays in the atmosphere for less time than carbon dioxide, its heat-trapping ability is 28 times more effective. And so the more methane that is released into the atmosphere, the hotter Earth becomes, resulting in more unpredictable and extreme weather. The good news is that since methane doesn't stick around too long, anything that is done to reduce the amount of methane released into the atmosphere has an immediate and positive impact.

SOMETHING FISHY

The Canadian farmer worked with his animal-expert friend Dr Rob Kinley to test how seaweed affected his cattle, and one of the findings was the reduction of methane in the cows' guts. After moving to Australia to work at CSIRO, Dr Rob continued researching the positive benefits of seaweed and discovered how, by adding seaweed to cattle feed, the cows not only produced less methane but also gained weight – which is a good thing in cows. With a 20% increase in the production of milk and meat as well as a substantial reduction in methane emissions, farmers and green investors jumped on the research to produce specialised cattle feed.

SQUAWK!
CSIRO stands for Commonwealth Scientific and Industrial Research Organisation.

RED IS BEST

Dr Rob Kinley tested about 30 different types of seaweed, and discovered one that topped the charts in methane reduction. While many seaweeds can reduce methane production in cow guts by 20%, the Tasmanian native red seaweed *Asparagosis* almost eliminates the production of methane altogether. It was such a great result that Dr Rob didn't believe it and thought his measuring instruments were broken. The reason this particular seaweed works so well is down to the amount of bromoform in it, which stops hydrogen and carbon bonding together in the cow guts, and so stops methane production.

FULL OF HOT AIR

With more than 1.5 billion methane-producing cows on the planet, it is imperative for the environment that seaweed-containing feed becomes the go-to for all cattle farmers across the globe. Because the seaweed effect is so great, even if just 10% of cattle farmers added seaweed to their cattle feed, it would have the same environmental impact as taking 100 million petrol-fuelled cars off the streets.

ECO TIP

To show your support for methane reduction, opt to buy low-methane beef if it is available. Otherwise, eat less beef and more vegetables. They really are good for you and require a lot less resources from the environment to grow.

THE GOOD NEWS

NATIONAL TREE DAY

One of the simplest things we can do to support Nature is plant a tree. With one small action you can help cool the climate, provide homes for native wildlife and green the future. Since 1996, more than 27 million trees have been planted by 5 million volunteers around Australia thanks to Planet Ark's National Tree Day campaign. National Tree Day has grown into Australia's largest tree-planting and nature-care event. Schools, councils, workplaces, community groups and individuals all dig in each year to make a difference in their communities.

EVERY DAY IS TREE DAY

Each year, Schools Tree Day is held on the last Friday of July, and National Tree Day on the last Sunday of July, but at Planet Ark we believe every day is Tree Day. Which is why we created Planet Ark's Seedling Bank, to give money to school and community groups to empower them to work on regeneration projects, such as the students at Warrawong High School, who cleared all the plastic and rubbish from the gully behind their school and used the funding to plant subtropical rainforest trees, shrubs and grasses. They also introduced a bee-habitat garden to pollinate the native trees as well as the fruits and vegetables growing on the school grounds and in the wider community.

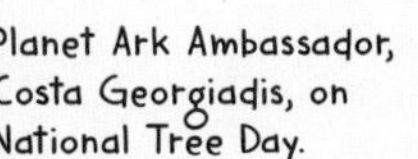

Planet Ark Ambassador, Costa Georgiadis, on National Tree Day.

TREES THAT HELP LOCAL WILDLIFE

At Howrah Primary School in Tasmania, students planted spiky shrubs, grasses and trees to expand the home of the threatened bandicoot, away from predatory foxes. They did this by planting the trees between one area of bandicoot habitat and another, creating what is called a wildlife corridor to help the bandicoots make the move.

DID YOU KNOW?

If you and your school or local community are inspired to spearhead an environmental project, you could find yourselves in another Planet Ark book! *Tree Talk* is a shout out to some of the important projects already undertaken by the Tree Day community with funding from The Seedling Bank. Join the eco-warriors and you might just see your name in print in a future edition of this inspiring book.

The Future

THE FUTURE

While we can't go back in time to change choices that have been detrimental to the planet so far, we can make better choices now for our planet's future. Because we can't exist without it. We need a future that gives back as much as it takes. A future that is curious about how Nature works to solve problems and takes inspiration from it. A future that safeguards Nature as much as humans. And it's not just about becoming an environmentalist or conservationist. It's about taking the time to do your research and using it to inform your choices in everything you do. In the products you use – or don't use. In the plants you plant – or don't plant. And in the waste you waste – or don't waste . . . Here are some stories of people who have already started, and who are sharing their knowledge to support others (including our government) in making choices that put safeguarding our environment at the top of the priority list.

THE WASTE HIERARCHY

While the world is still a long way from closing the loop to become a circular economy that has zero waste, the good news is that we are at least learning to manage that waste in a less harmful way. Even the way we dump rubbish in landfill has changed. We have moved away from open dumpsites in which waste was literally dumped into a big hole and left, and moved to a more managed system in which the landfill site has been designed to safely hold rubbish and its contaminants without any leaks. But there is so much more we can do to keep valuable resources in circulation, and a good place to start is by looking at the waste hierarchy.

The waste hierarchy is a scale from 1 to 5, with 1 being the best strategy that we want to do more of, and 5 being the worst strategy that we don't want to do very often.

REDUCE & AVOID	1
REUSE & REPAIR	2
RECYCLE	3
COMPOST	4
LANDFILL	5

The waste hierarchy is used around the world, and not only helps us to manage our waste responsibly but can also be used to inform the design of future products. For instance, if a material will end up in landfill because it can't be composted, recycled or reused, designers know from the start to avoid using that material in their products, turning a potential 5 on the hierarchy into a 1.

> **“Our planet’s alarm is going off, and it is time to wake up and take action!”**
>
> Leonardo DiCaprio,
> actor

THE GOOD NEWS
ECO-FRIENDLY IS BUSINESS-FRIENDLY

Businesses around the world are waking up to the realities of how the linear economy of the human cycle is unsustainable – not only for the environment, but for business, too. Constantly sourcing new materials is expensive, pollution makes people sick and so causes employees to take more leave, and taxes that businesses pay if they are a carbon-producing industry reduce profits. By designing processes that have zero waste and by reusing materials instead of buying new, the adoption of the circular economy is predicted to benefit Australia by $210 billion within 20 years.

THE ALL-ROUNDER

The circular economy is just as important for established businesses to adopt as it is for new businesses to start. Some of the circular practices that all businesses could implement include recycling and reducing waste, rethinking packaging and setting up services for reuse and repair. These practices have been proven to not only open up new areas in which businesses can make money but also improve brand image (how people perceive the business), reduce waste and support the wider development of sustainable services. Encouraging more businesses to do these things has a far greater impact on the environment than anything we can achieve as individuals.

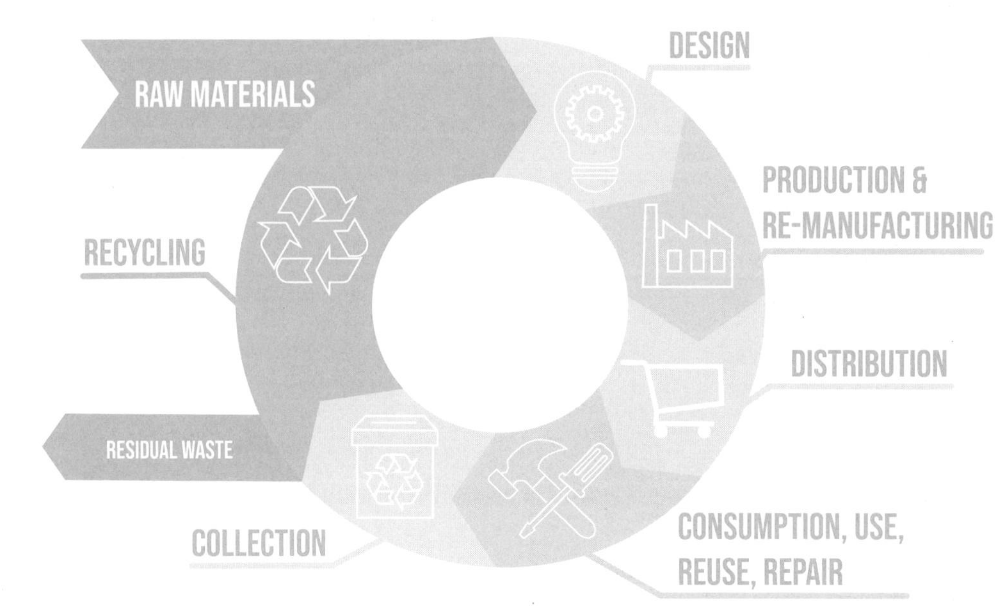

GREEN IS THE NEW BLACK

A circular economy is not only good for a business's bank balance, but also for its image. Many business owners have reported that the more sustainable business model of the circular economy means they're able to offer higher quality products thanks to their using more durable, high-quality renewable materials. This also has the added benefit of a happy customer, which means they keep coming back and will recommend the business to their friends. Lastly, research also suggests that employees are happy when they work for a business that prioritises sustainability.

EVERYTHING A CIRCLE

When businesses are circular, they are reusing resources, reducing waste and extending the lifespan of the products they create. As this becomes the norm and expands to more mass-market operations, it has a positive effect socially; it reduces the cost for consumers, improves customer experience and creates local, sustainable jobs in the resource management industry. Combined, the economic and social benefits of the circular economy positively impact the environment by decreasing the amount of greenhouse gas emissions, reducing strain on finite resources and minimising waste.

THE GOOD NEWS
SOLVING THE PLASTIC PROBLEM

Plastic is one of the biggest problems, because it is difficult and expensive to reuse or recycle, so it too often ends up in landfill, at the bottom of the waste hierarchy. Here are some of the creative ways that scientists and product designers are exploring options to avoid plastic in landfill.

THE BIG MICRO

We all know how plastic clogs our waterways and harms both wildlife and marine life, but there's more to it than that. While it takes a long time for plastic to completely decompose and not exist any more, it does fragment into something called microplastics, which are tiny pieces of plastic less than 5 millimetres in size. Because microplastics are so tiny, they can be easily ingested by accident. These tiny pieces of plastic have been found inside fish caught for eating, and so it is no surprise that we are finding microplastics in humans, too. Thankfully, the Seabin group (see pages 22–25) has been collecting data from the hundreds of tonnes of microplastics that it has removed from the water and are using that data in the world's first Microplastic and Ocean Health Research Lab based at the Australian National Maritime Museum in Sydney's Darling Harbour. The hope is that the data they collate and the information they extract will help to clean up the planet as well as inform new policies to prevent further plastic pollution.

BANNING

Banning single-use plastic items is one way of cutting down the amount of plastic we send to landfill. While we may only use items such as disposable plastic forks for a few minutes, those plastic forks can take centuries to break down in landfill. By ensuring all new products can be used more than once, we can better manage what we send to landfill and ensure we only use products that are reusable. If we don't make these changes, it is estimated that there will be more plastic by weight in our oceans than fish by 2050. And, for many single-use products, there are already alternatives made from paper, stainless steel, bamboo or glass. These products serve the same purpose but can be composted, recycled, or used multiple times, such as reusable bags for supermarket shopping, bamboo cutlery from takeaway stores, or glass cups and mugs at cafes.

BALANCING ACT

The reason we can't ban all plastics is because they are extremely useful and – newsflash – not all plastics are bad. Australian conservationist and keen scuba diver Dr Karen Raubenheimer has deep-dived into researching the management of plastic waste, and how it might be governed from a global perspective. Her work has helped inform discussions between countries on a treaty to reduce plastic waste, and it is in part thanks to her insightful research and advice that single-use plastics are being phased out in countries around the world. But, while she has seen firsthand the damage plastics are doing to our marine life in particular, she also acknowledges the benefits of plastics to our society. This is very much the case when you look at medical instruments, for instance. In the medical industry, plastic's strength, lightness, easy moulding and ability not to degrade over time are qualities that make it the perfect material for many medical tools and applications that are crucial for the health of patients. And that is not going to change. So Dr Raubenheimer's approach is to get rid of toxic and unnecessary plastics, and learn how to manage the useful plastics to prevent damage to the environment.

BANS ALREADY IN EFFECT

Most states and territories in Australia have implemented single-use plastic bans to achieve meaningful plastic waste reduction. These bans limit or completely remove the amount of single-use products available. Some of the already-banned single-use plastics include plastic bags, plastic drinking straws, cotton buds with plastic sticks, plastic bowls and plates, plastic cutlery, expanded polystyrene food and drink containers, and products containing microbeads, like face cleansers and cosmetics.

THE GOOD NEWS
ELECTRIC MOVES

Humans are more mobile today than ever before. From cars and planes to shuttle trips to the moon, transport is one of our biggest and most successful legacies. It is also one of the most environmentally destructive parts of our human world. Now that we understand the environmental costs of that success, bright sparks around the world have developed new technologies to reduce the negative environmental impact through using electricity to power our transport.

THE ENVIRONMENTAL IMPACT OF MOVING

Australians' love affair with the car is no secret, but the dominance of petrol-fuelled cars is an environmental disaster – especially with the rise in SUVs, which are large cars with large engines that require large amounts of petrol. The problem with petrol is that it comes from oil – a fossil fuel. Fossil fuels – oil, coal and gas – are not only limited resources but are a massive store of carbon. When they are burned to release their energy, all of that carbon is released into the atmosphere as carbon dioxide – a harmful greenhouse gas. Moving to cars that are powered by electricity removes those greenhouse-gas emissions from our roads.

SQUAWK!
In 1876, German Nicholas Otto invented the internal combustion engine that is still used in cars today.

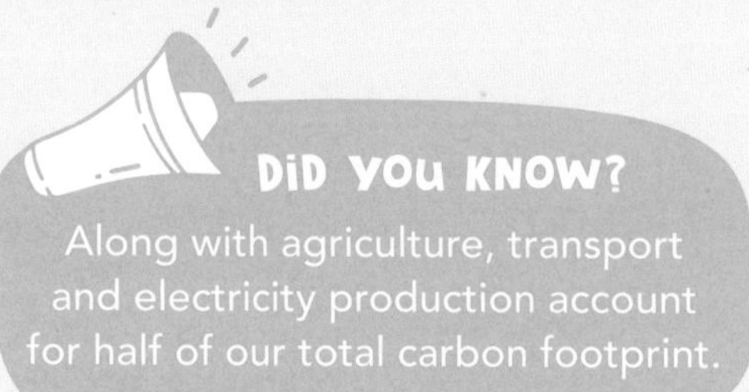

DID YOU KNOW?
Along with agriculture, transport and electricity production account for half of our total carbon footprint.

HOW CARS WORK

INTERNAL COMBUSTION AND ELECTRIC ENGINES

The internal combustion engine changed the human world and allowed it to develop at great speed. But, after 150 years of running our transport, the internal combustion engine is definitely due an upgrade to one that is circular in its operations, with zero waste. While the internal combustion engine is powered by what is essentially a controlled explosion that burns petrol and releases harmful gases through the exhaust, an electric vehicle emits no waste, and so is much more efficient because it doesn't waste any of its power in 'cleaning' toxic gases.

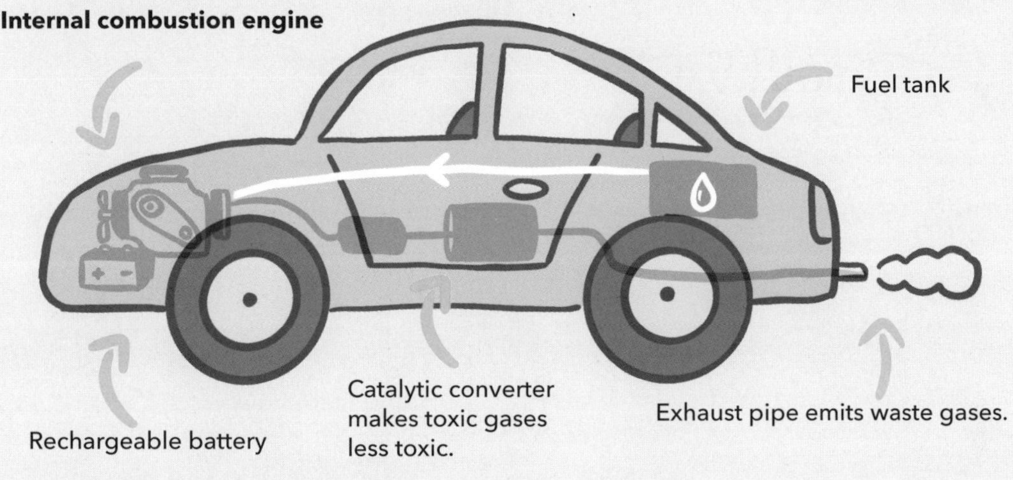

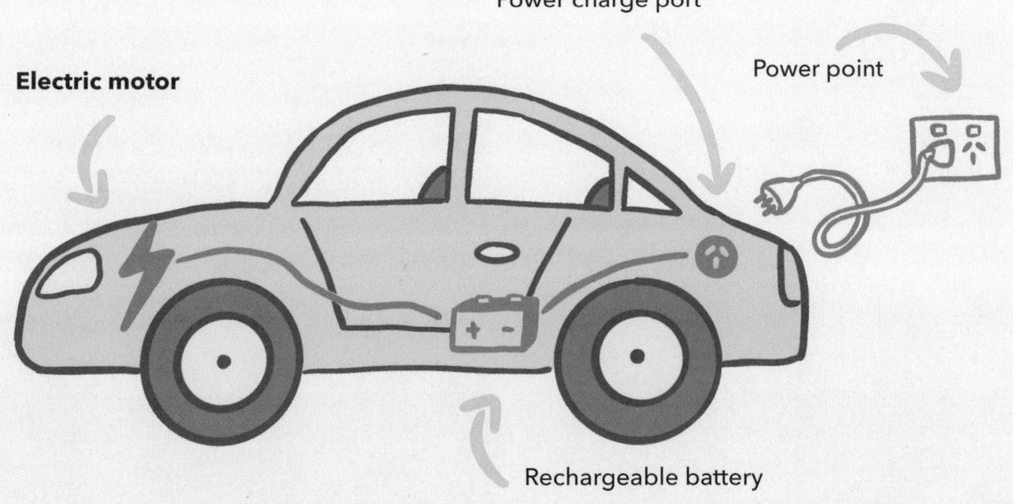

THE PAST DRIVES THE FUTURE

The electric car isn't anything new – from the 1830s when the electric motor was first conceived by Michael Faraday, crude electric vehicles were being trialled by resourceful inventors. And in the early 1900s, electric cars accounted for a third of all vehicles in the US. But a combination of factors around the development of petrol-fuelled cars and their mass production by Henry Ford, as well as cheap and prolific supplies of oil, led to the demise of the electric car and an explosion in the number of cars powered by the internal combustion engine. In the 1970s, when oil prices skyrocketed and electric vehicles were literally being driven on the moon, an interest in electric cars was reignited and car companies started investing once more in developing electric options. Fast forward another 20 years, and new regulations around pollution and emissions were requiring more efficient models to be manufactured. Toyota's Prius became the first mass-produced hybrid vehicle.

DID YOU KNOW?

Something that is hybrid is made from two different elements. A hybrid car uses two different types of fuel – such as electricity and petrol. When a hybrid car speeds beyond 50km/h and needs extra power, it switches from electric mode to combustion mode. This makes hybrid cars especially efficient around cities where they rarely reach high speeds.

ELECTRIFYING EVERYTHING

Whether you call it electromobility or e-mobility, the electrification of transport is on the rise. More and more people are making the conscious choice to buy environmentally friendly products, and this is beginning to extend to cars and other types of transportation. Electric vehicles have evolved in their technology to compete in power and speed with traditional options, and there are more electric vehicle charging points being set up in public spaces all the time. Electromobility describes not just cars but other forms of transport, too, including bicycles, motorbikes, scooters, trucks and buses, among others.

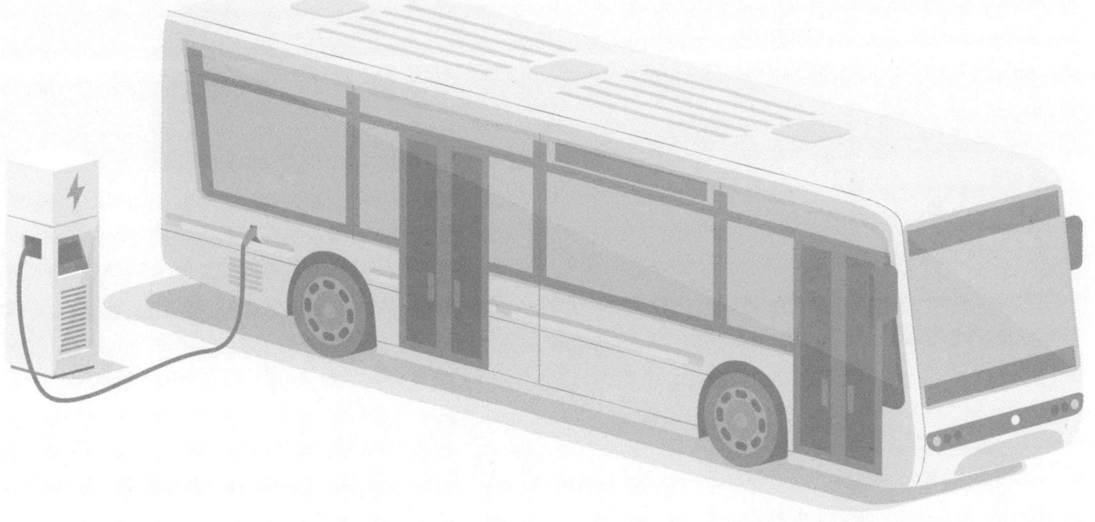

PROBLEM SOLVED?

Not quite. Electromobility is only truly circular and environmentally friendly if the electricity used to power vehicles comes from renewable sources like solar and wind energy. This means closing down coal-fuelled power stations and transforming the whole electricity grid to use renewable energy. Or, on a smaller scale, using on-the-spot renewable energy to power vehicle charging stations.

The Future

THE GOOD NEWS
SOCIAL MEDIA GOING GREEN

TikTok is a social media app that allows users to share and watch short-form videos, covering the silly and pointless as well as the serious and worthy, from funny memes to global news. Some 'eco-creators' set up EcoTok to showcase videos and content specifically about sustainability and the environment – and it is having an impact on those it reaches. More and more eco-influencers are now using the platform to share inspiration and tips on connecting with nature and living sustainably. And they have large numbers of engaged followers – the comments sections are filled with people sharing their own recommendations about gardening, sustainability, and a range of other eco-topics.

MEET KAYLAH

Kaylah Du Cane is one such eco-influencer. She has nearly half a million followers on TikTok through her account *environmental.education*. The young Victorian calls her account 'a sustainability diary', and it is full of videos showing how she makes eco-friendly choices through sustainable actions in everyday situations around her home. For example, one video shows how she composts vegies, while another shows how she grows new vegies from old ones. Did you know that to grow a pineapple, you just replant the top, spiky bit?! She also talks about the importance of making use of what we have around the house rather than buying new things all the time.

As you can tell, ive been collecting ...

environmenta... 10.5K

#regrow #howtogrowvegtables...

environmental... 7148

Thank me later #sustainability...

environmenta... 2934

environmental.educa...

SQUAWK!
An influencer is someone who has built their reputation as an authority in a specific area, and has a large and engaged social media following, making their posts influential and far-reaching.

INFLUENCE VS IMPACT

Eco-influencers are called that for a reason. They reach thousands of people with their videos. But does influencing lots of people actually result in impact? Could they be changing the world, one short, homemade video at a time? While the number of followers and likes doesn't mean people are actually acting in sustainable ways, the comments give more insight. For instance, on one of Kaylah Du Cane's posts about reducing waste when buying fruit and vegies, one of her followers commented:

"Since ur videos I have stopped putting my bananas in bags and I now choose the single ones :)"

This shows the impact of Kaylah's videos and is what we call behaviour change. Sometimes, it can be difficult to know whether people are actually making changes in their lives as a result of what they see on social media. Comments like this show that they are.

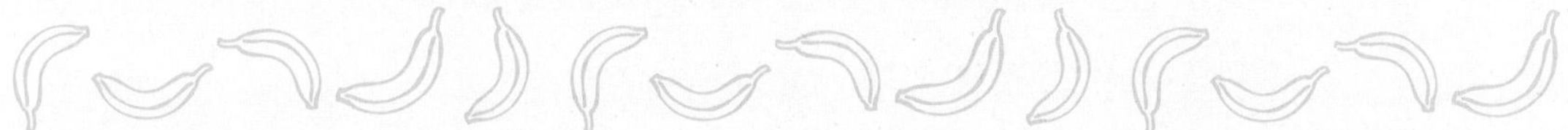

#NATUREISTRENDING

The engagement with environmental issues on TikTok isn't limited to comments. Many millennials and Generation Z are creating and sharing memes and other content. And it's popular! The hashtag *#nature* has 77.3 billion views (which is more than *#squishmallows*, just so you know). This content goes on to reach new audiences when reposted on other social media platforms such as Twitter/X and Instagram, increasing the impact.

DOING IT TOGETHER

A 2020 survey of Gen Z and millennials found climate change and protecting the environment was a top concern, both before and during the coronavirus pandemic. This follows the rise to fame of Greta Thunberg and the growth of Fridays for Future and other movements like Schools Strike 4 Climate.

An Xiao Mina is the author of the book *Memes to Movements*, and has studied social movements on social media. She says that while the most visible thing is the meme, what is less noticeable are the communities that are being built, the stories being shaped and the impact that might help younger generations create effective change.

INSPIRE, INVOLVE, IMPACT

EcoTok may not save the planet on its own, but it is having an impact when it comes to the decisions people make in their daily lives, as well as making bigger ripples such as helping young people get involved in climate action.

BE A GOOD-NEWS HERO

Everything we do in the world has an impact. No matter how big or small our footprints are, what we do matters.

The future is quite literally in your hands, and it is up to YOU to continue the good work. To start your own innovations and ideas hubs. To learn lessons from others' mistakes, and to make lots yourself – that is what Nature does through evolution, which just goes to show: mistakes really are part of a natural progression.

So we dare you. Try something different to make a change that is better for all.
All the world, that is.
Human and Nature.
Together.

You've got this!

GLOSSARY

accountability – taking responsibility for your actions and their consequences.

ARL (Australian Recycling Label) – an on-pack label providing simple recycling information for packaging on products sold across Australia and New Zealand.

biodiversity – the huge variety of living species, including plant and animal life, that are all interconnected and interdependent.

biofuel – a liquid, solid or gaseous fuel, made from natural matter over a short period of time. One example is ethanol.

carbon footprint – an estimate of the total amount of greenhouse gases released into the atmosphere over a certain period from the actions of a person, organisation, product or event.

carbon offset – an action that reduces the amount of carbon dioxide in the atmosphere (such as planting native forests), to make up for gases being released somewhere else.

circular economy – a system that ensures resources are continuously in use and never wasted. The opposite of a linear economy.

coral – marine animals that are related to sea anemones that often build reefs. Coral polyps are jellyfish-like animals that create hard skeletons to live in from calcium in the seawater. They attract algae, which gives them their colourful appearance.

coral bleaching – the process in which coral lose their vibrant colours, turning white due to high ocean temperatures that makes them expel the colourful algae.

coral reef – an underwater structure of a community of coral that provides habitat for a biodiverse marine ecosystem.

cycle – a recurring series of events or actions that come full circle and are then repeated many times in the same order.

decompose – the natural process through which materials break down.

eco-friendly – describing products, events and services that are designed to have little or no harmful impact on the environment.

economy – the way people spend and make money through goods and services.

ecosystem – an interacting community of living things in their environment.

energy – the sun is the source of all energy on Earth. Living things absorb the sun's energy and convert it into different forms of energy, such as glucose, to grow. Energy is never lost, it is simply transformed. Humans have developed ways to harness energy and use it for specific purposes, such as to power transport and create electricity.

equator – an imaginary line that circles Planet Earth around its centre and marks the point where the Northern Hemisphere and the Southern Hemisphere meet.

erosion – when land materials such as rocks and soil are gradually worn away by natural forces such as wind or water.

fibre – a long, thin, threadlike strand of material. Natural fibres, such as cotton and silk, come from plants and animals. Synthetic fibres, such as polyester, were invented by humans. Fibres can be spun together to make thread, or woven into a fabric and used to make clothing.

fossil fuel – coal, gas and oil are all types of fossil fuel; an energy source formed from the buried remains of dead plants and animals over millions of years. The energy is released from fossil fuels by burning them.

green – being environmentally friendly; a word to describe the way companies or people strive to conserve Earth's resources, showing concern for the environment.

greenhouse gas – a type of gas that naturally occurs in Earth's atmosphere and acts like a greenhouse to trap some of the sun's energy on Earth, making it warm enough for life to thrive. Too many greenhouse gases in the atmosphere due to human actions increases the greenhouse effect, causing more of the sun's energy to be trapped on Earth and warmer temperatures such as with global warming.

igneous rock – one of the three primary rock types, it is the rock mostly found on Earth's surface. It is formed when magma (molten rock or lava) cools and becomes solid.

industrialisation – the process in history where technology transforms a nation's economy, improving production and creating goods and services.

landfill – a place where waste is buried in large amounts under the soil.

linear economy – the opposite of circular economy; a system that has a beginning and an end, in which raw materials are turned into products, used and then discarded as waste.

metamorphic rock – one of the three primary rock types, it is rock that has gone through change due to heat and pressure, which has caused its structure to change.

microscopic – objects or living things too small to be seen by the human eye alone unless magnified through a microscope.

mining – the process of extracting materials and minerals of value, such as coal, gold and iron, from Earth.

native – a word used to describe a plant or animal that belongs to a specific and unique environment.

non-recyclable – something that cannot be recycled.

oil spill – when tankers or pipelines carrying oil (a fossil fuel) break down and spill oil into the environment, which can be catastropic for wildlife. Oil floats in water, and so destroys coastal habitats that it washes up on, as well as marine life.

old-growth forest – a naturally occurring forest whose trees have grown over a long period of time, not disturbed or damaged by humans.

photosynthesis – the process where plants use sunlight, water and carbon dioxide to make energy to grow, releasing oxygen at the same time.

pollution – the addition of harmful substances (pollutants) into the environment, which can affect the health of wildlife habitats and humans for years. The three main types of pollution are air, water and land.

polyester – a type of synthetic (human-made) fibre, usually made from oil and woven into a fabric that is used in clothes and other textile products.

power station – a place that converts the energy from fuel into electricity.

PREP (Packaging Recyclability Evaluation Portal) – an online tool, specifically for use in Australia and New Zealand, in which the raw materials of packaging can be entered to assess how recyclable a packaging design is. This information is then used to inform the information printed on the Australian Recycling Label (ARL) on products.

rainforest – a forest of mostly evergreen tall trees that receives heavy rainfall. Rainforests are found in the tropical zone (see page 60), are Earth's oldest living ecosystems and, as such, have an immense diversity of wildlife.

reef (see also coral reef) – a ridge or bar of rock or coral near the ocean surface.

recyclable – a word to describe material that can be processed for reuse.

responsible sourcing – also known as ethical sourcing, it is a process of collecting or purchasing materials (such as timber) that comply with environmental and human rights regulations.

runoff – the excess liquid (such as water) that runs over the land and into nearby creeks, streams or ponds.

sedimentary rock – this is one of the three primary rock types. It is produced over millions of years when sediment (tiny fragments of broken-up rocks) is compressed into layers of rock.

species – a classification of a group of organisms that share a similar biology and can reproduce naturally.

sustainability – the management of natural resources over a long period of time, ensuring a resource is never used up or damaged beyond repair.

synthetic – a word used to describe a material or substance created by humans.

textiles – a piece of material spun or woven from *fibres*, such as cotton, silk or polyester.

Tropic of Cancer – also called the Northern Tropic, it is an imaginary line that humans use to measure distances around the globe. It sits 23½ degrees north of the equator, and is the most northern part of Earth where the sun can be directly overhead.

Tropic of Capricorn – also called the Southern Tropic, it is an imaginary line that humans use to measure distances around the globe. It sits 23½ degrees south of the equator, and is the most southern part of Earth where the sun can be directly overhead.

tropical – a word to describe the tropics, which is a region on Earth around the equator that extends north to the Tropic of Cancer and south to the Tropic of Capricorn. The climate in the tropics is characterised by continuously warm termperatures and lots of rainfall.

waste – a product or substance no longer wanted or in use. Waste is discarded and thrown away, often by being buried under soil in landfill.

waterway – a natural body of water that flows to the ocean, such as rivers and creeks.

weathering – the process through which rocks on Earth's surface are broken down, eroded or dissolved as a result of the weather, such as wind, rain or a change in temperature.

wildlife corridor – a narrow area of an animal's habitat, usually native vegetation, that connects two or more larger habitats together.

yield – in agriculture, a measurement of the amount of crops or product produced on a particular area of land.

Established in 1992,
Planet Ark is one of Australia's most respected and trusted environmental organisations. We are focused on solutions and making positive environmental actions accessible to everyone.

Positive actions are at the core of every decision we make. We are defined by what we are for, not what we are against. Our goal is to build a better world - one where humans not only live in balance with nature, but help it to thrive.

PLANET ARK PROGRAMS

- National Tree Day
- The Seedling Bank
- National Recycling Week
- Australian Circular Economy Hub
- Recycling Near You
- Business Recycling
- Australasian Recycling Label
- Cartridges 4 Planet Ark
- Batteries 4 Planet Ark
- Make It Wood
- Planet Ark Power
- PodCycle
- Product Stewardship Hub

PICTURE CREDITS

Preliminary Pages

p4: Turtle/Alfmaler/Shutterstock.com; **p5:** Eucalyptus leaf/Woodhouse/Shutterstock.com; **p7:** Human hands holding globe/Danielala/Shutterstock.com; Lightbulb/svtdesign/ Shutterstock.com

Chapter 1 – Blue Planet

pp12-13: Ocean/avmedved/Stock.Adobe.com; **p13** (& in logo throughout chapter): Turtle /Alfmaler/Shutterstock.com; **pp14-15:** Australia and Oceania/ixpert/Shutterstock.com; **p16:** World map/ Maxger/Shutterstock.com; **p17:** Water cycle/Sarah Wiecek/Planet Ark; **p18:** Greenhouse effect/Sarah Wiecek/Planet Ark; **p19:** Ocean currents/Sarah Wiecek/Planet Ark; **pp20-21, 24, 34, 36, 37:** Marine life/Drawlab19/Shutterstock.com; **p22:** Floating plastic bottles/Vivid Pixels/Stock.Adobe.com; **p23:** Seabin / Sarah Wiecek/Planet Ark; **p25:** World globe/Malchev/Shutterstock.com; **p26:** 'Josh' aerial/The Ocean Cleanup; 'Josh' on-deck/The Ocean Cleanup; **pp26, 32, 35, 44, 46, 49, 57, 59, 60, 61, 126, 128, 130:** Cockatoo illustration/Sarah Wiecek/Planet Ark; **p27:** World map illustration showing ocean garbage patches/Elime/Shutterstock.com; **p28:** River interceptor /The Ocean Cleanup; Sunglasses/The Ocean Cleanup; **pp30:** Two boys work together/Bettermind Graphic/Stock.Adobe.com; **pp31,126:** Children's toys /JosepPerianes/Shutterstock.com; **pp32-33:** The Turtle Tribe images x 5/supplied by Ned Heaton, The Turtle Tribe; **pp33:** Notepad paper sheets with pen/SpicyTruffel/Shutterstock.com; **p34:** Diver with coral spawning/Coral_Brunner/Stock.Adobe.com; **p36:** Loggerhead turtle/Miroslav Halama/Shutterstock.com

Chapter 2 – The Power of Nature

pp38-39: Tropical leaves /MG Drachal/Shutterstock.com; **p39** (& in logo throughout chapter): Eucalyptus leaves/Woodhouse/Shutterstock.com; **pp40-41:** Misty forest/Angyalosi Beata/Shutterstock.com; **p42:** Balance stones against the sea/Aleksandr Simonov/Shutterstock.com; **p43:** Rock Cycle/Sarah Wiecek/Planet Ark; **p44:** Oxygen Cycle/Sarah Wiecek/Planet Ark; **pp44, 46, 126, 128:** Megaphone/mhatzapa/Shutterstock.com; **p45:** Carbon Cycle/Sarah Wiecek/Planet Ark; **p46:** Nitrogen cycle/Sarah Wiecek/Planet Ark; **p47:** Mountains & icebergs/TheBlackRhino/Shutterstock.com; **p49:** Soil layers/Sarah Wiecek/Planet Ark; Microbes/Vasilinka/Shutterstock.com; **p50:** Carbon storage/Sarah Wiecek/Planet Ark; **p51:** Symbols x 7/Sarah Wiecek/Planet Ark; **p52:** Sam Vincent with wheelbarrow/supplied by Sam Vincent; **p53:** Cow illustration/Sarah Wiecek/Planet Ark; Compost cartoon/N.Savranska/Shutterstock.com; Grass silhouette/kstudija/Shutterstock.com; **pp54, 57:** Tree silhouettes/Robert Adrian Hillman/Shutterstock.com; **p54:** Grass silhouette/kstudija/Shutterstock.com; **pp55, 61, 63:** Bugs/Lexi Claus/Shutterstock.com; Fruit/dizdino/Shutterstock.com; **p56:** Seeds & leaves/Flaffy/Shutterstock.com; **p57:** Svalbard Global Seed Vault/hopsalka/Stock.Adobe.com; Wollemi Pine trunk image/AlessandroZocc/Shutterstock.com; **p58:** WA Forest Alliance protest group/supplied by WA Forest Alliance; **p59:** Carnaby Black Cockatoo in artificial hollow/Jane Hammond; Grandma Tingle Tree/Joanna Nelson-Hauer/Shutterstock.com; **pp60-61:** Leaves/MG Drachal/Shutterstock.com; **p62:** Animal hole cross-section/Sarah Wiecek/Planet Ark; **p63:** Giant Gippsland earthworm/supplied by Dr Beverley Van Praagh; **p64:** Fossil fuels / Sarah Wiecek/Planet Ark; **p65:** Highway photo/puyalroyo/Shutterstock.com

Chapter 3 – The Human Cycle

pp66-67: Globe world map /Vdant85/Stock.Adobe.com; **pp68-69:** Walking people blur/IRStone/Stock.Adobe.com; **p70:** Sydney skyline/Greens87/Shutterstock.com; **p71:** Take,Make,Waste/Sarah Wiecek/Planet Ark; Pile of garbage /Tribalium/Shutterstock.com; **p72:** Circular economy icon/Deemerwha/Stock.Adobe.com; **p73:** Circular economy bins/Sarah Wiecek/Planet Ark; **p74:** Circular economy graphic/Sarah Wiecek/Planet Ark; **p75:** Green bamboo/enjoynz/Stock.Adobe.com; Wheelie bin/Sarah Wiecek/Planet Ark; **p76:** Loganholme solar array/supplied by Logan City Council; **p77:** Solar panel recycling/ Sarah Wiecek/Planet Ark; **p78:** Biochar images/ supplied by Logan City Council; **p79:** Cow/Dudarev Mikhail/Stock.Adobe.com; **p80:** Solar panel/Sarah Wiecek/Planet Ark; **p81:** Child doing waste audit/Sarah Wiecek/Planet Ark; **p82:** PREP logo/Supplied by Packaging Recylability Evaluation Portal; Recycle eco tag template/

Denys Holovatiuk/Stock.Adobe.com; **p83:** PREP diagram; Sarah Wiecek: Planet Ark; **p84:** Products with ARLs/HCurdie; **pp84-85:** ARL symbols & cartoon/Sarah Wiecek/Planet Ark; **p86:** C4PA used toner cartridges/Planet Ark; **p87:** C4PA toner pave/Planet Ark; **p87:** Lousy Ink products/Oliver Reade; **p88:** Worn Up images x 3/Supplied by Annie Thompson; **p89:** Soccer jersey/tondruangwit/Stock.Adobe.com; **p90:** Yellow flipflops/david_franklin/Stock.Adobe.com; Yellow swimming goggles/Ruslan Grumble/Shutterstock.com; Healthy school lunch/Timolina/Shutterstock.com; **p91:** Plastic recycling code/Liena/Stock.Adobe.com; **p92:** Swan Song photo/Supplied by Mina DeBris; Megaphone/mhatzapa/Shutterstock.com; **p93:** Ploys Design products/ Supplied by Carin Van Gunsven & Gerhard Sandker; Inflatable pool toys (vector)/unturtle/Stock.Adobe.com; **p94:** Burdock Seed/Sarah Wiecek/Planet Ark; **p95:** Sustainable timber/Sebastian/Stock.Adobe.com; Butterflies/ONYXprj/Stock.Adobe.com; Flat cars set/MicroOne/Stock.Adobe.com; Ladybird/Lexi Claus/Shutterstock.com

Chapter 4 – Social Innovation

pp96-97: Green city landscape/sarymsakov.com/Stock.Adobe.com; **p97** (& in logo throughout chapter): Human hands holding globe/Danielala/Shutterstock.com; **pp98-99:** World Environment Day concept/Pcess609/Stock.Adobe.com; **p100:** Pink piggy bank/Monkey Business Images/Shutterstock.com; **pp100, 101** Gold and silver coins/VectorPlotnikoff/Shutterstock.com; Big yellow mining truck/Parilov/Stock.Adobe.com; **pp101, 107, 109:** Ladybird/Lexi Claus/Shutterstock.com; **p102:** Bottle deposit/Ivan Zelenin/Stock.Adobe.com; **p103:** Carbon credit vector icon/Calin/Stock.Adobe.com; **p104:** Set of bottles/gassh/Stock.Adobe.com; **pp104, 107, 108, 111, 112:** Black cockatoo/Sarah Wiecek/Planet Ark; **p105:** Gouldian Finch/Sarah Wiecek/Planet Ark; Foregrounds of woodlands/Robert Adrian Hillman/Shutterstock.com; **pp106, 110, 111, 113, 115,** Megaphone/mhatzapa/Shutterstock.com; **p106:** Scissor and comb icon/popicon/Shutterstock.com; **pp106-107:** Sustainable Salons images – foil bales, sunglasses, hair donation; hair bundle/supplied by Lucy O'Keeffe; **p107:** Closeup of newspapers/STILLFX/Shutterstock.com; Slick industry oil fuel/Ilya Andriyanov/Shutterstock.com; Bottle of poison/Martial Red/Shutterstock.com; **p108:** Airplane flying around planet earth/Zoya Zhuravliova/Shutterstock.com; Grass detail/kstudija/Shutterstock.com; **p109:** Spices and herbs/primiaou/Shutterstock.com; Ice cream (food theme vectors)/Ola_view/Shutterstock.com; Farmwall/supplied by Farmwall Pty Ltd; p**p110, 111:** Kuno fridge cross-setion and images/supplied by James Dyson Award; Trophy (football objects vectors)/balabolka/Shutterstock.com; **pp112, 113:** Cow eating seaweed, red seaweed & cow illustrations/Sarah Wiecek/Planet Ark; **p114:** Warrawong High School students/Aristo Risi; **p115:** Costa Georgiadis/Adam Crews/Planet Ark; National Tree Day logo/Sarah Wiecek/Planet Ark; Howrah Primary School students/supplied by Planet Ark; Eastern Barred Bandicoot/169169/Stock.Adobe.com; Tree silhouette/PinkPueblo/Shutterstock.com

Chapter 5 – The Future

pp116-17: Sun and waves/puckillustrations/Stock.Adobe.com; **p117** (& in logo throughout chapter): lightbulb/svtdesign/ Shutterstock.com; **pp118-119:** Futuristic buildings & trees/sanju/Stock.Adobe.com; **p120:** Waste hierarchy/Sarah Wiecek/Planet Ark; **p121:** Recycle symbol/ImageFusion/Stock.Adobe.com; **p122:** Circular Economy/ Planet Ark; **p123:** Circular Economy hand-holding/Deemerwha/Stock.Adobe.com; **p124:** Magnifying glass/Sarah Wiecek/Planet Ark; **p125:** Scuba diver Karen Raubenheime image/supplied by Karen Raubenheime; **p126:** Carbon footprint/m.malinika/Stock.Adobe.com; **p127:** Petrol & electric cars/Sarah Wiecek/Planet Ark; **p128:** Electric car charging/Yellow duck/Stock.Adobe.com; **p129:** Boy & scooter/Varta Scooter/Unsplash; Electric bus/petovarga/Stock.Adobe.com; **p130:** Kaylah Du Cane TikTok profile image/supplied by Kaylah Du Cane; **p131:** Banana illustrations/dizdino/Shutterstock.com; **pp132-133:** cityscape with greenery image/Kien/Stock.Adobe.com

Endmatter

pp144-141: Rainforest & valley/HCurdie